RESIDENT BITCHES & KILLER DIVAS

Enjoy!

Annie Wall

Annie Wall

Dedication

This book is dedicated to the one person who is always there for me, no matter what.

The one who encourages me, the one who cheers me on. The one who listens to my sometimes crazy ideas and laughs with me daily.

There is no other person in my life like him, my husband, Dale. Thank you for your support and love.

Acknowledgment

I would like to thank Amazon Publishing led by Emma Baker who was with me throughout this process. I cannot begin to thank her and her staff enough.

I would also like to thank my husband Dale and my daughter Amberlin who always encourages me to continue my writing journey.

I would like to thank my many friends who have read my first book and can hardly wait for my second book to be published. I have enjoyed our many conversations about my characters and what they will be up to next.

A big shout out to my good friend Candy Marsh who is always full of smiles and positivity.

Preface

Fergus Quimby, retired homicide detective, has moved to Summers Bay after years on the job. His plan was to fish and live a quiet life.

He bought into a senior retirement community and found out that single women outnumbered the men. Beverly Johnson, the founder of the Diamond Divas,' has plans for him.

Lily Bright comes to visit her former partner when the two of them end up in the middle of a homicide investigation. The local sheriff is only interested in waiting out his retirement. The investigating duo is at it again, where everyone is a suspect.

This is the second book in a series. It is laced with humor and the antics of single senior women. Women who will do anything to get what they want, even kill.

This is a work of fiction. The characters, places, and events in this book are fictitious and the work of the author's very wild imagination. Any similarity to events, locals, or real persons, living or dead, is purely coincidental and not intended by the author.

Table of Contents

About the Author

Annie Wall is from Oregon and retired to Arizona with her husband, Dale. They live in a senior retirement community with their toy teddy bear poodle, Lucy. Where they enjoy the many amenities that are available to them.

Besides enjoying the Arizona lifestyle and the sunshine. She keeps busy with dance classes and the karaoke club. She sings and dances with her group, "*Golden Girls & Silver Guys*" ." They put on a one-hour variety show for free at retirement communities in the west valley of Phoenix.

Annie enjoys reading, painting, writing, and spending time with family and friends who have become family. She is now writing the third book in this series, "*The Burns Brothers Hotter than Ever.*"

Chapter 1:
Apartment #110

A warm breeze moved through the sheer white curtains that hung from the open patio door of apartment #110. The voice of Frank Sinatra singing "Strangers in the Night" played repeatedly on a CD player in Blanche Smith's small living room. The music floated out to the patio area by the pool, where windchimes kept in time with the music.

Two champagne flutes sat on the breakfast bar where they waited to be filled, a strawberry nestled at the bottom of each flute. An unopened bottle of cheap champagne sat in a bucket of melted ice.

From the small kitchen, you could see into the bedroom where Blanche lay on the bedroom floor beside her Queen-sized bed. She had one fuzzy black high-heeled slipper on, the other on the floor by the bottom of the bed. Blanche wore a black baby doll nighty with a sheer robe trimmed in black feathers. The nightstand drawer emptied onto the bedroom floor next to her body. Among the contents were lotions, oils, creams, KY jelly, condoms, fuzzy handcuffs, and a dildo that somehow found its way into Blanche's mouth. Her head was tilted back, and her eyes opened wide, looking toward the ceiling.

Blanche had been widowed for eight years. She was starting to get involved with the singles clubs, starting with "*Sassy Singles Who Like to Mingle.*" It was a social club that hosted dances, dinners, and happy hours. Blanche was a beautiful lady who quickly became very popular with single men. There were more eligible women than there were men who resided at 'Sunshine Village by the Sea.' Several of the single women noticed all the attention Blanche had received. It was obvious that they didn't care much for her. She had become their biggest competition. One might say they were jealous of her.

She recently became a member of the 'windchime club.' A club that was not talked about out loud. You had to be invited to be a member. If you were looking for a good time, you would put purple windchimes out by your patio, inviting company in by leaving a door unlocked. The fun part was you never knew who would show up. A 'good time' meant anything from watching a movie or having dinner to a sexual encounter.

It was a housekeeper who found Blanche Smith's body. There wasn't any sign of blood. No sign of anyone else in the apartment. Nothing looked disturbed other than the nightstand drawer that had been dumped out onto the bedroom floor. The housekeeper let out a scream that could have woken the dead, except Blanche didn't wake up.

The sheriff arrived. He didn't seem to be in a hurry . He knew the body wasn't going anywhere. Sheriff Sam, as the locals called him, was in his late fifties. He was a wiry fellow who moved to this coastal town a few years back to wait out his time until retirement. Summer's Bay seemed to be the perfect mid-sized community to do just that. The crime rate was very low in this sleepy little town.

Sheriff Sam entered apartment #110 looking official in his starched uniform, his gun belt hung low on his hips. He looked around as he walked toward the bedroom.

Residents gathered in the hallway, trying to find out what was going on. The sheriff left the front door of the small apartment open. He entered the bedroom, where Blanche was sprawled out on the floor. He shook his head as if in disbelief at what he saw. He turned and walked back into the living area. He looked around as if he had lost something and was trying to find it. He walked over to the sliding door that was open and closed it. The sheriff then walked back into the bedroom, where he was doing the same thing, looking for something.

Residents, trying to see what they could, pushed their way up to the open front door. They watched the sheriff as he walked around the small apartment. One resident, Hazel, whispered, "I think he is looking for clues." Edna whispered back, "How would you know what he is looking for?"

"I watch that crime TV channel. This is what they do, trust me."

Sheriff Sam didn't seem to notice anything out of the ordinary. Blanche replaced the carpet with hardwood right after she purchased the apartment. There didn't seem to be forced entry or any sign of footprints. As far as the sheriff was concerned, he didn't see any sign of a struggle. Nothing was turned over other than the nightstand drawer. Sheriff Sam stood over the body . He looked down at Blanche and shook his head, " Tsk, tsk."

The medical examiner arrived with his assistant to transport the body to the morgue. They laid a black bag beside the body. Sheriff Sam stood by. He watched as the body was placed inside the bag.

Sam scratched his head, "This looks to be a suicide to me; I don't see any sign of foul play. Case closed!" he said with a curt tone. As he turned to walk away, the medical examiner raised his eyebrows as he looked at the sheriff. "So, we have death by dildo? Is that right, sheriff?" Giving him a quizzical look. The assistant started to laugh.

"It appears so. HEY!" he shouted at the assistant," there is nothing funny about suicide. Nothing is disturbed other than the nightstand drawer. It looks like she planned this out."

The medical examiner closed the body bag with a tug of the zipper. The bag was lifted onto a gurney. Shaking his head as he rolled it out the front door of apartment #110. The residents made room for them to get through as they headed toward the lobby. He whispered to his assistant, “Unbelievable!”

“Boss, he’s not serious, is he?” the assistant whispered back.

“I’m afraid he is.”

Residents watched in shock as the gurney rolled down the hallway toward the front doors. They all shuffled their feet as they followed behind the medical examiner. They watched with concern as the body was placed into the back of an old white station wagon. The whispers grew louder as the medical examiner drove away with Blanche.

Sheriff Sam walked out to the lobby. He called out to the residents by the front entrance, “Can I have your attention, folks?” Their voices turned to dead silence. All eyes looked toward the sheriff, who was standing in the lobby. He made a stance placing his hands on his hips, “As you already know, the resident of apartment #110 has passed away. There is nothing more to see, folks.” A woman called out, “How did she die?” “I’m sorry to say it was suicide. You can all get back to whatever it is you do here. Good day.” Sheriff Sam walked out the front door toward his police cruiser.

The residents looked at each other in disbelief. One whispered, “Suicide? Not Blanche! I don’t believe she would do that.” Beverly Johnson overheard that remark as they walked away from the front entrance, “I don’t like to speak ill of the dead . However, that is one less to compete against when it comes to the single men,” she said with a smirk on her face.

Sondra Miller walked up beside Beverly and stopped, “Beverly, you should be ashamed saying something like that!”

"Oh, come on, Sondra, you know the truth when you hear it. Don't go acting all prissy on me now. Blanche was getting back into the game of things; you didn't like her any more than I did."

Sondra put her hands on her hips as she leaned toward Beverly, "Maybe we all were a bit envious of Blanche. She was not only beautiful, she was sweet too. You need to look in the mirror at yourself before you go and judge someone. As my mother used to say, 'Beauty is skin deep . However, ugly goes down to the bone.' Think about that!" Sondra turned and walked away from the group.

Beverly looked surprised at what Sondra said to her as she walked with her group of followers, "I wonder what crawled up her ass and died." The others all giggled at that remark. Hazel and Edna followed the group down the hall. Edna whispered to Hazel, "Looks like someone needs to do a bit of housekeeping around this place." Hazel smiled and nodded in agreement. Beverly didn't take well to being challenged, especially by Sondra.

You could call Beverly Johnson the leader or head honcho of her group of followers. They referred to themselves as 'Diamond Divas,' Beverly, and the girls thought that name made them sound fun as well as classy.

In the days that followed, apartment #110 was emptied and cleaned, ready for the next buyer, who happened to be a retired homicide detective. Detective Fergus Quimby was from Springfield, a small town a couple of hours west of 'Summers Bay.'

The gossip pipeline was abuzz with rumors and half-truths. Sara Lee, who everyone called 'Cookie' heard the rumors and knew she shouldn't listen to them. However, she found them more entertaining than the National Enquirer magazine.

Cookie bought and moved into her apartment #100 a little over a year ago. Blanche and Cookie had become fast friends. Blanche was ready to get back into the dating pool. She confided in Cookie about the 'Windchime Club,' the club supplies their members with purple windchimes so they could be identified by other club members." Cookie didn't think that was a good idea and told Blanche about her concerns.

"Blanche, are you really okay with someone coming into your apartment, not knowing who it will be? Stop and think about all the dangers. What if there is a pervert? A murderer? What if you get a horrible disease? Have you thought about this at all?"

Blanche just laughed at Cookie, "Not to worry, I'm safe. This club is just inside our complex . It isn't open to the outside."

Cookie wasn't convinced, "You are way too trusting. Why not do a website for senior singles?"

Blanche, still chuckling, "Cookie, that is where the perverts and murderers hang out. It's much safer here in our group than any internet dating service."

Cookie remembered her conversation with Blanche and then said out loud, "See, Blanche, I was right, wasn't I?" A tear rolled down Cookie's cheek. "Who am I going to talk to now? Why didn't you listen to me, Blanche ? Why?"

It was moving day for Fergus. His dark blue sedan was packed with all his worldly belongings. His prized fishing poles and tackle box were packed inside a coffin-like plastic container that was attached to the roof of his sedan. He was ready to make the two-hour drive to his new home in Summers Bay. Retirement had finally arrived, and not a day too soon. He looked forward to relaxing on his patio with a beer after his arrival.

The drive to the coast always seemed to take longer than the drive back to Springfield. This time it was a one-way trip. Fergus made a stop at a small grocery store to pick up a case of beer and a few other items . He thought he might need to get settled in.

Fergus pulled his sedan into the covered carport space marked #110. He sat behind the wheel of his car for a few moments when Brian Carpenter walked up.

"Hey neighbor, need some help moving in?"

Fergus stepped out of his car . He smiled at Brian Carpenter. "Hey Brian, that would be great. You showed up at the right time."

Fergus and Brian had met the day Fergus bought his new condo. Brian was a retired police officer. The two men had a lot in common. The men each carried an armload into the apartment. Fergus was excited to see his new recliner and counter stools had arrived. He looked toward the bedroom and saw his new bed had arrived as well. "Looks like I won't have to camp out in the recliner tonight," Fergie smiled as he unloaded his case of beer and groceries onto the kitchen counter. "Hey Brian, just put those things on the bed. I'll take care of them later." The men finished unpacking Fergus's sedan.

"Fergus, is this everything? Or do you have to make another trip back to Springfield?"

"Brian, I am a man of simple means. What I have here is everything I need. If I need anything else, I can pick it up later in town. Are you ready for a beer yet? You look a little thirsty." The men laughed as they took their drinks out to the patio.

The gossip pipeline was up and running. "There's a new single man that just moved into apartment #110." Residents were buzzing. "Officer Brian seems to know him." "I wonder if he knows about what happened to Blanche?"

Brian and Fergus were relaxing on the patio, enjoying their second beer, when the doorbell rang. Fergus got up from his chair . Brian smiled and said, "And so it begins."

"What are you talking about?"

"You will find out soon enough."

All the single ladies were excited to meet this new man that moved into their village. They each had their own ideas on how they would make that happen. Beverly Johnson was the first to ring Fergus's doorbell. Beverly was known to be very forward and outgoing. When she had her mind made up about something, she followed through. She was now focused on Fergus.

Fergus answered the door, beer in hand. Beverly, a tall curvy redhead, smiled when she saw this tall, good-looking 'single' man.

"Can I help you?" Fergus asked.

Beverly held out an apple pie, "I made it myself." Fergus smiled at her.

"It's a housewarming gift for you. I'm Beverly Johnson . I live upstairs in #201."

Fergus took the pie, "Thank you, Beverly, I'm Fergus Quimby."

Beverly moved toward Fergus, pushing her way inside. He stepped backward .

"Let me set this down," he said as he sat the pie on the countertop. Beverly continued to move forward, closer to Fergus.

"Fergus, that's Scottish, isn't it?" she said in a sultry way.

Fergus takes another step back, "Yes, I was named after my grandfather." Beverly reached her hand toward Fergus and touched his arm.

"You know what that means, don't you?" as she rubbed his bicep.

"No, what does it mean?"

"Your name means 'man of force,' I like that," she said in a low sultry voice. Beverly inched her way closer to Fergus, "My, you must work out . You've got some nice muscles." Beverly giggled as she pushed her body up against his. Fergus backed away from this pie-making siren of a woman as Brian walked in from the patio.

"Ah, Beverly, I see the welcoming committee has arrived."

"Oh, hello Brian, I didn't know you were here." She backed away from Fergus.

"Obviously," Brian said with a half-smile.

"Fergus, it was so nice to meet you. I'll be seeing you around, I'm sure," Beverly said in a whispered voice, then blew him a kiss as she stepped toward the front door.

Fergus turned toward Brian, "Welcoming committee?"

Brian took a swig from his beer, "Beverly Johnson is the leader of a group of single ladies who call themselves 'Diamond Divas.' I've heard others call that same group 'Satan's Saints' and a few other names."

Fergus grabbed himself another beer, "And what do you call them, Brian?"

Brian chuckled, "I don't really call them anything. If I had to name that group, I would call them 'Maneaters.' Both men laughed.

Beverly noticed Roxanne James walking toward her in the hall. Beverly smiled as she passed Roxanne, "Don't get your hopes up . He's all mine."

"We'll see about that," Roxanne said in a curt tone. She continued past Beverly as she carried her homemade carrot cake. She whispered, "*Bitch.*" Beverly stopped and turned toward Roxanne, "I heard that!" Roxanne kept walking, "Good!" Beverly felt the anger welling up inside her . L*ooks like I might have to teach that one a lesson or two.*

No sooner had Beverly left when the doorbell rang again. Fergus opened it up to a dark-haired petite lady holding a cake. She opened the door wider with her foot, "May I come in?" She stepped inside the doorway, "Hello, gentlemen, I thought I would come by and bring you..."

Before she could finish her sentence, Fergus completed it, "A housewarming gift." "How did you know I was going to say that?" she said with a smile in her voice. Fergus then pointed to the apple pie.

"Just set it on the counter." Roxanne placed the cake on the counter, pushing the apple pie out of the way and off to the side. "I made this from scratch . I hope you like carrot cake." Fergus stood by the door, "Actually, it's one of my favorites." Roxanne walked toward Fergus, "Let me introduce myself. I'm Roxanne James. I'm in apartment #123 . If you look from your patio, I'm across from you. Now tell me your name, darlin'?"

"Fergus Quimby." Fergus wasn't used to being the center of attention.

"Interesting name Fergus. I won't stay . I don't want to get in the way of whatever it was you two men were doing before I got here." Roxanne walked toward the front door. Fergus opened it for her.

"Thanks for the cake . That was very neighborly of you."

"You are very welcome, Fergus . Let me know how you love it." She smiled at Fergus and winked. Fergus closed his door while Brian broke out into laughter.

Fergus looked at Brian, "What the hell was that all about?"

"You're fresh meat, my friend. Single men are far and few in-between, especially in our age group.

"What's the joke, Brian?" Brian was still trying to contain himself.

"They call her Foxy Roxie. This is just the beginning, my friend."

"How do I make it stop?" Fergus said with a quizzical look.

"Just enjoy the food, don't act interested unless you are. It should die down on its own. Right now, you are in the sight of every single woman in this place."

"Oh, lucky me," Fergus said in a flat tone, "I'm going to have my meals delivered to my condo for a while."

Brian grabbed another beer.

"Sit back and enjoy the attention. If you hide, they will find you." Fergus and Brian headed out to the patio.

The view from the patio was nice. You could see the pool and hot tub area. There was a walkway around the pool where walkers would walk early in the morning and in the early evening.

It was midafternoon. The walkway going around the pool was busy with single ladies who were waving at Brian and Fergus as they passed his patio. The men sat in their chairs and raised their beer bottles as they walked by. Fergus shook his head at the parade, " Are they out here for the exercise? Or are they just checking us out?"

Brian smiled, "My friend, I was checked out when I moved in. This is all about you." Brian finished his beer and stood up, "I'd love to stay," he laughed. "However, I'm going to go. I have a few things I need to get done. This is your parade." Fergus walked Brian to the door.

"Thanks for helping me move in . I'll see you later."

Fergus stepped into the hallway as a little red poodle ran toward him. A blonde-haired lady was calling, "Lucy, Lucy, you get back here." Fergus picked up the cute little dog.

"I believe this is Lucy?"

"Yes, thank you." Lucy really liked Fergus. She cuddled up in his arms as if she knew him.

"You must be married." The lady blushed.

"No, I'm not." Fergus handed Lucy back to the blonde-haired lady.

"What made you think I was married?"

"I thought you might be married because you're not in the parade outside."

"Oh, that, no, I don't participate in all that craziness. Let me introduce myself. Hi, I'm Sara Lee . Everyone around here calls me 'Cookie.'

"Nice to meet you, Cookie, I'm Fergus Quimby, and I'm in #110."

"Yes, I know. My friend Blanche lived there before you. Sadly, she passed away. We were very good friends."

"I'm sorry for your loss, Miss Cookie."

"Thank you. It was nice to meet you."

"Same here."

Cookie carried Lucy back toward her apartment. Fergus rubbed his chin as he watched Cookie walk down the hall.

In the days that followed, the parade out by the pool had died down. The food deliveries had stopped. Fergus was beside himself, wondering what to do with all the food that was piled up on his countertop. There were two dozen chocolate chip cookies, an Angel Food cake, a peach pie, an apple pie, a carrot cake, homemade bread, chicken soup, and three casserole dishes, all made from scratch, so he had been told. "All I need now is a Partridge in a pear tree, and I'll be set." He laughed at his own joke.

Chapter 2:
Cookie and Lucy

Fergus was an early riser; he still wasn't used to being retired. He was meeting Brian for breakfast in the dining room. Fergus locked the door to his apartment as he started down the hall. He could see a group of single women walking toward him.

Cookie had just opened the door to her apartment. She had taken Lucy out for her morning walk.

The women were getting closer. They waved and called out, "Good morning, Fergus." In a sing-song voice.

Fergus wasn't used to all this attention. He gave a quick wave and walked into apartment #100 behind Cookie. Lucy ran to Fergus to greet him. Cookie turned and saw Fergus behind her . He quickly shut her front door.

"Oh, my, you startled me, Fergus!"

"I'm sorry to barge in on you, Cookie, but…."

Just then, there was knocking on the door, "Fergus, we know you're in there . Come out . We just want to get to know you." The knocking continued.

Cookie walked over to her door and called out, "Go away . If he wants to talk to you, he will look for you. Leave him alone."

"Oh, come on, Fergus, how are we ever going to talk if you keep hiding from us?"

Cookie recognized that voice to be Beverly Johnson. "Beverly, take a hint and beat it!"

The knocking stopped as suddenly as it began. You could hear the women talking to each other as they walked away.

Fergus took a handkerchief out of his pocket and wiped his forehead. "Mind if I hide out for a few minutes? I was on my way to the dining room to meet Brian for breakfast."

Cookie shook her head, "I can't believe how they're acting! They did the same thing to Brian when he moved in. I don't know if they are desperate or just plain horny! Maybe both!"

Fergus laughed, "They are like the paparazzi, following me everywhere."

"Have a seat . I'll fix you a cup of coffee."

Fergus sat down in an easy chair. Cookie brought him a cup of hot coffee. "I hope you like it black; I don't have any cream." She smiled as she handed him a mug.

"Black is fine, thank you."

"Why don't you do what Brian did to stop all this madness?"

"What did Brian do?" Fergus asked with a surprised expression on his face.

"I'm surprised he hasn't told you. He told them if they didn't stop harassing him, he was going to get a restraining order out on each and every one of them."

"And that worked?"

"Yep!"

"I'm going to have a chat with Brian when I see him."

Fergus finished his coffee and thanked Cookie for hiding him out.

"The coast is probably clear by now. Do you want me to walk you to the dining room?"

"No, I can make it there on my own. Thanks again."

"Thanks for stopping by," Cookie smiled as she held Lucy.

"I'll let myself out."

Fergus walked into the dining room. Brian waved at him from a booth. Fergus slid into the booth and gave Brian his deadpan look.

"Hey bud, what's up? I almost left; I didn't think you were going to show up."

"I would have been on time if I wasn't being stalked by every single woman in this place. Well, not everyone. Cookie had to hide me out."

"Still after you, are they?" Brian chuckled.

"I heard from Cookie that I need to threaten them with a restraining order like Brian did in order to get them to stop."

Brian smiled, "Oh, that? Yeah, that worked for me. I figured you would handle it your way."

"Brian, I'm a retired homicide detective. I'm not used to people chasing me . I'm the one that usually does the chasing."

Brian laughed; he raised his hand to get the attention of the waitress.

"Good morning, gentlemen . What can I get you?"

Fergus looked at the menu. "I'll have coffee and the Denver Omelet with pancakes, please."

"And for you, sir?"

"I'll have coffee with cream, eggs over easy, hash browns, and sausage, thank you." Brian handed the waitress his menu.

"Coming right up," she said with a smile as she took their menus.

The men enjoyed small talk along with their coffee. Fergus looked around the dining room and noticed some familiar faces. There was one man who always sat in the back corner booth facing the doorway to the dining room. He was a tall, slender fellow who wore thick-framed black glasses . He had a pocket protector that held several pens. His white hair was cut short and combed neatly. He always sat alone every time Fergus saw him.

The waitress returned with their breakfast order. "Enjoy your breakfast, gentlemen."

"Hey Brian, what's up with that guy in the back corner who always sits alone?"

"Oh, that's Eugene. He is always reading something on atomic energy or scientific something or other. He's a loner and seems to like it that way. I think of him as a 'watcher.' Notice where he sits . He can keep an eye on everything that's going on and everyone who comes and goes."

"Interesting . Do you know what he used to do for a living?"

"I've heard he was some kind of engineer. Not a railroad engineer, he was one who sat in a cubicle for 8 hours a day. I've heard he isn't much of a conversationalist. I guess when you work alone like he did, it would be hard to relate to a group of people."

"Is this guy married?" Fergus asked as he took a bite of his omelet.

"I believe he was at one time . I heard he bored her to death." Brian smiled and sipped his coffee.

Fergus nearly choked on his coffee. He wiped his mouth with a napkin. "Really? She died?"

"Yeah, no kidding. I made the died of boredom part up. I thought you might like that."

"Why aren't the single ladies chasing after him?"

"Come on, Fergus, take a good look. The guy has huge feet and wears the same old white tennis shoes with those white socks that are halfway up to his knees. You never see him wear anything but those old tennis shoes. He is tripped up by his own feet. Watch him walk on the carpet. He shuffles his feet as if afraid he's going to trip and fall. If you were a single lady, would you chase after him?"

"Well, not when you put it that way," Fergus smirked.

"I hear he goes to all these seminars about different illnesses that he doesn't have but might get." Brian chuckled, "Nothing like being prepared."

"Is he a pot smoker? He sounds terribly paranoid."

"I guess if you really wanted to know more about him, you could go over and meet him."

"I think I will hold off on that one for a while." Fergus enjoyed his omelet, "I can't get over how good the food is here. If I had to cook for myself, I would lose weight. Now I have to be careful not to put too much on."

The men finished their breakfast with a second cup of coffee.

"Can I get you to help me hang my television on the wall sometime?"

"Sure, let's do it now . It's supposed to be a nice day. I'd like to go out to the pool later."

The men walked back to Fergus' apartment. This time the hallway was quiet. They entered the apartment, and Brian looked over toward the counter.

"Fergus, what are you going to do with all that food?"

"I put some in the refrigerator already. Do you want to take some back to your place?"

"I'll take a couple of things off your hands. Do you have some freezer zip bags? You might want to freeze some of this stuff so it doesn't go bad."

"Yeah, I'll do that. First things first, I would like to get this television hung."

Brian lifted one end of the TV to see how heavy it was. "Great, you have the brackets up; the rest shouldn't take long. What size screen is this?"

"58 inch. It will just fill that space on the wall."

Brian was right. Hanging the television was done quickly with both men on the job. Fergus thanked Brian for his help. Brian left with a casserole, pie, and a dozen cookies.

Fergus decided to take a walk to the pier and check out where he was going to spend some of his time fishing. It was about a 15-minute walk from 'Sunshine Village.' He put his hands in his jacket pockets to keep them warm. There was a bit of a chill in the air. He was glad he decided to wear a light jacket. Several people were fishing off the pier when he arrived. He walked out toward the end to see if anyone was having any luck. He stopped and asked a man, "Are they biting this morning?" The man looked over at Fergus as he shook his head, "Not so much today . Yesterday I caught a few." Fergus wished him good luck and headed back home. On his walk back, Fergus noticed a bait and tackle shop not far from the pier. He knew where he would be buying his live bait.

The hallways seemed quiet, which was a relief. He thought to himself, *maybe those women have found someone else to pester for a while. I could really use the break.*

Fergus fumbled with his keys as he tried to open his apartment door. Once inside, he rubbed the palms of his hands together, trying to warm them up. The TV weatherman assured the residents of Summers Bay that warmer weather was forecasted for the afternoon.

Fergus walked over to his patio door and noticed Eugene sitting out by the pool with a book under an umbrella. He was wearing shorts with huge pockets that looked to be stuffed with things he might need for his pool outing. Just like Brian had said, Eugene was wearing tall white socks and those huge white sneakers. He was wearing a hat that shaded his face with white cream smeared on his nose and cheeks. Fergus thought to himself, *maybe he dresses like that on purpose to keep the women at bay.*

Fergus relaxed in his recliner and watched the happenings outside by the pool. Walkers were out walking. There were a few single ladies who seemed to be enjoying their morning walk . As they passed Fergus's patio, they waved.

Fergus dozed off. He woke up to the smell of perfume. He sat up, looked around, and didn't see anyone. He got up and checked his door. It was locked. He walked into his bedroom; nothing was disturbed. He looked at the kitchen clock and realized he had slept for an hour. He walked over to his patio window. Looking out, he noticed Eugene was gone, and a few sunbathers were out.

The afternoon warmed up as promised by the television weatherman. Fergus decided to sit out on his patio with a cup of coffee. He people-watched for a while. He felt like he could finally relax. He noticed a lady in a white dress. She walked toward him; her shoulder-length silver hair was windblown. She waved and smiled as if she knew him. Fergus watched as she walked up to his patio gate.

"Hi, I'm Lacey Martin. I wanted to wait before I dropped by to introduce myself. I don't take part in the 'She Devils' antics. They call themselves 'Diamond Divas.' That's a laugh. Mind if I join you?"

Fergus smiled, "Why not? Come on in."

Lacey sat in the empty chair on Fergus's patio, "Hey, do you have another one of those?" she pointed at his coffee.

Fergus got up from his chair, "Sure, let me get you one."

Lacey brushed her hair back away from her face. Fergus handed her a coffee mug. "Thanks" She took a sip, "Ah, this is nice . You know you have a great view. Blanche loved it here. It's sad how she died."

Fergus was interested in what Lacey had to say, "Tell me, I knew the previous owner had passed away. I was never given or have I heard of any details."

Lacey sat back, relaxed in her chair. She set her mug on the table between them. "I knew Blanche. She was a sweetheart. She and Cookie were very close. Those two were always together. Blanche had recently decided to get into the dating scene. Her husband passed away a few years back. The gossip is she was a member of the 'Windchime club.' Blanche was expecting company the night before she was discovered by the housekeeper."

Fergus was intrigued by what he was hearing, "What is the 'Windchime club'? I haven't seen that listed with the other clubs that are offered here."

Lacey sipped her coffee, "It is said you must be invited to join. It's an exclusive club. When you're a member looking for company, you put purple windchimes out on your patio, leaving a door unlocked. Company can be anything from a movie, dinner, whatever you are interested in, sex included," Lacy shyly smiled.

Fergus sipped his coffee, then rubbed his chin, as he always does when he is thinking. "Are you saying Blanche had invited someone over for, as you call it, 'company'?"

Lacey nodded her head, "Yes, Blanche was lonely, and she was new to the club. Our Barney Fife of a sheriff, called her death a suicide. Sheriff Sam likes things to be quiet here in our little town. He is waiting out his retirement. He doesn't know that we know his little secret. Residents stood outside the open front door when the Medical Examiner asked, 'so we have death by dildo?' Several of us heard him say that. We were all shocked by that remark."

Fergus looked concerned, "Seriously? You heard that?"

"Yes! I was as shocked as you are now."

Fergus sat his coffee mug down on the table. "Interesting, Lacey . You do know that I'm a retired homicide detective?"

"Yes, that is what I heard, and I thought you should know these facts. Blanche didn't kill herself. I hope you can get to the bottom of this."

Fergus frowned, "Lacey, did you hear me say the word 'retired'? This case belongs to the local authorities."

"Fergus, I had hoped you would feel differently once you heard some of the details. I know there is more to this so-called suicide. Thanks for listening anyway, and thanks for the coffee." She sat her empty mug down on the small table.

Lacey left as quickly as she had arrived. Fergus thought about what she told him. I'll talk to Brian about this later . I'm sure he knows something about this.

Chapter 3:
Medical Examiner's Office

Blanche's body lay in refrigeration, unclaimed. Dr. Eric Thompson was Summers Bay's medical examiner. He decided to do his own detective work. Sheriff Sam had been of no help with this case whatsoever. '*Lazy son of a bitch*' he thought to himself, "Kelly, would you make a few calls for me?"

"Sure, Doc."

Kelly, Eric's assistant, made a call to the Sheriff to see if he had any more information on Blanch that could help them find her family.

Kelly hung up the phone. She looked at Eric, "I swear our sheriff isn't interested in doing his job!"

Eric shook his head and replied, "And you're just now figuring that out?"

"I'll call over to 'Sunshine Village,' maybe they can help with locating her next of kin."

The medical examiner's office is not a busy place. In fact, business has been slow. Dr. Thompson wasn't taking the cause of death the Sheriff gave seriously. He wanted to find a relative that would give permission for an autopsy.

The phone rang at 'Sunshine Village.' "It's a wonderful day at Sunshine Village, Malissa speaking . How can I help you?"

"Hello, this is Kelly Anderson from the medical examiner's office. Is there someone there that can assist us in finding a relative of Blanche Smith?"

"Why yes, I can help you with that. I sold Blanche her condo. I have her paperwork. Can I put you on hold while I search for it?"

"Yes, of course," Kelly replied.

Kelly waited while she listened to elevator music on hold.

"Kelly?"

"Yes, I'm still here."

"I have one relative listed, her niece Darcy Smith. She lives in Springfield. Would you like her phone number?"

"Yes, that would be wonderful."

"Are you ready? Its 843.555.9832"

"Thank you, Malissa, you have been a great help."

Kelly hung up the phone. "Eric, we have a phone number for a niece who lives in Springfield."

Kelly and Eric high-fived each other. Kelly picked up the phone and made the call to Darcy Smith.

"Hello, may I please speak to Ms. Darcy Smith?"

"Yes, this is Darcy . To whom am I speaking ?"

"My name is Kelly Anderson . I'm with the medical examiner's office in Summers Bay. Are you a relative of Blanche Smith?"

Darcy swallowed, "Has something happened to my aunt?" Her voice started to shake.

"I'm so sorry I am the one to tell you, especially over the phone. Your aunt passed away, and she is here with us at our office. Would it be possible for you to come and make a positive identification?"

"Yes, I'll be there within a couple of hours. I need to call in at my office and let them know I'll be out for the day."

"Wonderful, we'll see you later."

Kelly hung up the phone.

"Doc, the niece will be here in a couple of hours."

"Good work, Kelly. Now with her consent, we can find out what really killed Blanche."

Darcy arrived at Summers Bay, Medical Examiner's Office, that afternoon. She was greeted by Dr. Eric Thompson and his assistant Kelly Anderson.

"I'm glad I was able to get here before you closed for the day. It was an easy drive, not much traffic on the road." Feeling nervous, Darcy shook Dr. Thompson's and Kelly's hands.

Kelly looked concerned for Darcy, "Are you ok?"

Darcy nodded yes, "I'm fine . I never thought I would have to do something like this."

Dr. Thompson opened the drawer that held the body of Blanche Smith. He then pulled the sheet back that covered Blanche's face. "Is this your aunt?"

Darcy covered her mouth with her hand. She nodded her head, "Yes, that is my aunt Blanche. What happened to her?" Her voice was shaky; a tear ran from her eye down her cheek.

Doc Thompson covered Blanche's face and gently pushed her back into the refrigeration drawer.

Doc Thompson put his hands in his white doctor's coat pockets, "According to our sheriff, it was suicide."

"And according to you, Dr. Thompson, what did my aunt die from?"

"In my opinion, I don't believe it was suicide. I would like your permission to do an autopsy to find the cause of death."

"Yes, yes, of course, you have my permission. Why would the Sheriff call it suicide?"

Kelly smirked, "Because he's an idiot and doesn't want to do his job. That is my opinion . Please don't quote me."

Dr. Thompson tries to keep his composure after Kelly's remark, "She has her opinion, and I have mine. I feel there is something deeper that we can figure out once we do an autopsy. Thank you for making the trip over here . We will keep you posted once we have the findings. I'll need you to sign off for the autopsy."

"Yes, of course. I look forward to your call. Thank you both."

Darcy was still shaken from seeing her aunt pulled out of a drawer and covered up with a sheet. She got into her SUV and started her drive back to Springfield.

Dr. Thompson walked over to his desk, removed his white coat, and hung it on a hook, "We have a busy day tomorrow. We can finally find out what is going on with our guest."

Kelly hung her white coat up on a hook by her desk, "Yes, I'll be ready."

"Kelly, you caught me off guard calling Sheriff Sam an idiot to Darcy. It was hard to keep from laughing."

"Hey Doc, I'm sorry it slipped out accidentally on purpose . What can I say? "Kelly smiled.

"Let's get out of here . We have a full day tomorrow."

***

The next morning

Kelly and Doc Thompson arrived early, about the same time. "Good morning," Kelly called out as she shut the door to her Jeep.

"Yes, it is," Doc called back.

There was a chill in the morning air as Doc Thompson and Kelly made their way inside the M.E.'s office. Things had been slow in Summers Bay, which wasn't unusual. This was a place where people came to retire . Deaths were usually due to old age. There hadn't been a murder in the last 10 years. Occasionally there would be a car accident, even those were far and few in-between.

Doc Thompson and Kelly put on their aprons and gloved up as they began to prepare for the autopsy. The body was moved from refrigeration to a gurney. Kelly rolled it over to the autopsy table. The instrument tray was set up next to the table. The sheet had been removed; the body was ready for the first cut. Kelly handed Doc Thompson a scalpel. He made the standard 'Y' incision starting at the shoulders and down to the belly button. This cut made it easy to fold the skin flaps back to expose the body's major organs. The organs were removed one by one and weighed. Kelly charted as Doc called out each organ's weight. There is a standard weight for each organ. If one weighs more or less than the standard weight, that can indicate a possible disease that will have to be checked out more thoroughly. Samples were taken of each organ along with blood and urine. The organs were then placed back into the body's cavity, not in any specific order, since the body would no longer need them. The brain was exposed and examined, along with a sample taken. The body was then placed back into refrigeration.

Samples were ready to go to the lab for analysis. "This shouldn't take too long to get the results back. I'm curious to see what the samples will tell us. Everything looked pretty good. I did notice there had been evidence of a past heart attack . A stent had been put in place. Other than that, I didn't see anything out of the ordinary."

"I'm curious as well, Kelly replied.

"Let's get these samples over to the lab."

Doc Thompson gathered the samples and placed them in a container to be taken over to pathology . He made a call for a courier, "I put a rush on them . Until then, we wait. With business being slow, we should get them back shortly."

"Doc, I hate it when you say it like that," Kelly replied.

"What?"

"You know, when you say business is slow, it sounds creepy."

"What's so creepy about that?" Doc asked with a chuckle.

Kelly shivered, shaking her shoulders, " Ewe! It gives me the creeps! I can't explain it," She shivers again.

Doc laughed out loud, "Kelly, you're going to have to get used to that if you're planning on staying in this business."

"I know," she said in a monotone voice, "I love what we do, helping people and giving family closure and all. I just feel weird waiting for customers." she shyly said.

"You'll get used to it , I promise. Let's take a break . We both deserve it. Kelly and Doc cleaned up their work area, which didn't take long, and left for the day.

Chapter 4: "Strangers in the Night" by Frank Sinatra

That fateful night

Blanche was nervous and excited all at the same time. She put her favorite Frank Sinatra song on her CD player . It fit the evening she was preparing for. She placed a bottle of Korbel champagne in a bucket of ice to keep it chilled. Everything seemed to be in place. This would be her first encounter with someone from the windchime club. Not knowing what to expect sent a chill of excitement through her. The mood was broken when the phone rang.

"Hello."

There was no answer . She could hear someone breathing on the other end.

"Hello, Cookie, is that you?"

Still no answer.

"Hello, if you're not going to talk, I'm hanging up."

She then called Cookie.

"Hello."

"Hey, Cookie, did you just call me?"

"No, why?"

"It must be someone making a prank call. There was no answer, just breathing."

"Blanche, do you want me to come over and stay with you?"

"No, I'm fine. Thanks for the offer."

"Do me a favor and lock your doors," Cookie said with a concerned voice.

"I will. I'll talk with you tomorrow."

Cookie hung up the phone. *That's odd . I wonder who is making prank calls to her.*

Blanche set champagne flutes with strawberries on the counter, "There, that looks perfect." She said with a smile. She walked into the bedroom and put on her black sheer feathered robe over the black baby doll she bought for this occasion. She slipped on her feathered slippers to match. She then reached for a box on the top shelf of her closet that held the purple windchimes. She opened the box and slowly held them up. She walked toward her patio and placed them on a hook outside the slider door, leaving it open by a few inches. Blanche walked toward her bedroom. She put on a dab of her favorite perfume, 'White Shoulders', before her company arrived. It had been a long time since she had been held by a man. She wasn't sure if this evening would lead to a sexual encounter . She was ready if it did, especially if there was mutual attraction.

She heard her slider door open. Her heart skipped a beat, "I'll be right out." Her back was to the bedroom door. She set her perfume bottle down. She heard footsteps come into her bedroom. She turned to see someone dressed in black. He grabbed her. She tried to scream, but instead, it was a cry so quiet, a breath, a whisper, then she went limp.

The intruder laid her down on the floor. He knelt to see if she was ok. She wasn't breathing. Panic set in, not knowing what to do. He looked around the room, then pulled the nightstand drawer out and dumped it on the floor. *This wasn't supposed to happen.* Seeing the contents from the drawer, he picked up a dildo that rolled by Blanche's head and shoved it into her mouth down her throat. He stood up and paced back and forth. He turned and walked toward the closet. He bent down and looked inside the dark space. He stood and then paced some more. Everything was neat. He decided not to make it look like a robbery. *This wasn't supposed to happen. I just wanted to scare her.* He walked back toward Blanche . He stood over her body. He looked down at her, and his hands started to shake. He turned toward the door and left the same way he came in. *This was an accident; how could this happen. She just collapsed.*

He was careful not to be seen going back to his condo. When he removed his clothes, he noticed his pen was missing. *Maybe I dropped it outside, that's it, I'm sure it's outside.* He tried to convince himself of that thought. He then put all the clothing he wore into a garbage bag. He would take it out to the dumpster the following morning with the regular trash. His hands were still shaking. He kept thinking the same thing over and over again . *This wasn't supposed to happen.* He looked out his patio window to see if anyone was out there. He didn't think he was seen. Overcome with regret. *I just wanted to scare her. I wanted her to think the windchime club was dangerous and quit. She didn't need to be involved in that club. She wasn't like the rest of them.* He poured himself a glass of wine and sat by the window, hoping no one saw him. Trying to compose himself with each sip he took.

The following morning is when Blanche is discovered by the housekeeper. He had to go and be part of the group that was looking for answers. If he didn't go or wasn't seen, it would look suspicious. His mind raced, hoping he didn't leave anything behind in her apartment. *I had gloves on . They are in the trash with the rest of my clothes. I know there won't be any fingerprints.* He heard the garbage truck emptying the dumpsters out back. He was starting to feel better.

Sheriff Sam arrived, taking his time as he always does. *He won't find anything. He doesn't like working. I don't know how he even keeps his job.*

The sheriff tried to calm the residents. He told them to go back and do what they were doing. Everything was under control. He was relieved to hear the sheriff called Blanche's death a suicide. He felt relieved . He was right . He didn't leave anything behind to be found.

Chapter 5:
Sunset Sisters

The sun was setting in Summers Bay. The word was out to meet at Beverly Johnson's apartment #201 for wine and girl time at five O'clock.

Beverly was setting out wine glasses, plates, and forks along with a cheese tray. She was ready for the single ladies she called, 'Sunset Sisters.' This was a club at 'Sunshine Village.' If you wanted to join, you were directed to contact Beverly Johnson . She was the President. It was more like a gossip club and do what Beverly told you to do club. Beverly had quite a few followers, which made her job easy.

The single ladies started to arrive, bringing a bottle of wine to share. Beverly made sure everyone had a glass of wine.

For the first fifteen minutes, the ladies mingled; chatter filled the small apartment. Beverly stood by the table where the cheese tray was. She tapped a fork on her wine glass to get everyone's attention.

"Ladies, ladies, may I have your attention, please. We have a few things to go over then you will be able to ask questions. Afterward , we can get back to our wine, cheese tasting, and conversation."

All the ladies had wine in hand, ready to hear what Beverly had to say. This was a once-a-month meeting, and not everyone was in attendance for this one. Roxane James was the secretary.

"Okay, ladies, let's get to the meat of this meeting. As you all know, there are more of us single ladies here in 'Sunshine Village' than single men. We just had two men move in. Gary Hart and Fergus Quimby both are from Springfield. I know some of you have already met Fergus. I must say he is a catch!" Beverly said with excitement in her voice, "I have already called dibs! So don't any of you get any ideas. Gary recently lost his wife, so I would say he is lonely. You can set your sights in his direction. If you are feeling a little desperate, you can always check in with Eugene. "There were "Boo's" and a few "ewes" after that remark.

"Come on, ladies, don't forget about Brian . He is single and a retired police officer. He might have kept his handcuffs." Beverly smiled and gave the ladies a wink. Laughter filled the small apartment.

Sondra Miller decided to call Beverly out. She had enough of Beverly bossing everyone around, "Hey Bev, you say you have dibs on Fergus, is that right? "Beverly turned toward Sondra. She raised an eyebrow as she looked Sondra in the eye, "Yes, that is right. We made a connection when he moved in. Like I said, he is mine, so stand down."

Sondra scoffed. "What if he doesn't want you?" Beverly took a sip of her wine, then wiped the corner of her mouth with a napkin, "Oh, he wants me alright . He just doesn't know it yet."

Sondra laughs, staring right back at Beverly, "So you think just because you eye- humped the detective and waved your magic silicone tits in his face, you think he's yours? That's not a connection, maybe for you, it's a connection, but I'll bet you he isn't one bit interested in you!"

The room filled with a few “Oohs.” Edna called out, “Ouch!” Snickers, along with laughter, trying to be held back. One thing Beverly wouldn’t stand for was being made fun of . Oh, she could dish it out . She just couldn’t take it when it came her way. Beverly could feel her face getting red as her temper was rising, “Quiet ladies!” Beverly snapped. “Sondra, you are out of line! Your ass must be jealous of all the shit that is coming out of your mouth! Do you remember me asking for your opinion? Well, me neither!”

Sondra looked around the room as she stood up, “are all of you going to follow Beverly around? Do what she says? I am my own woman. I will not take orders from her! If you’re with me, I’m leaving. Stay if you want to be one of her minions because that is all you will ever be.” Sondra walked to the kitchen counter and grabbed the bottle of wine she brought. She stopped in front of Beverly, “I hope you choke on your own nasty tongue.” She then headed toward the door.

“Wait!” Roxanne James called out, “I’m going with you.” “I’m coming too” Lacey Martin stood. They followed Sondra’s lead and grabbed their bottles of wine.

Beverly looked toward the door, “If you walk out that door, your memberships will be canceled! Don’t come back!”

Sondra stopped by the door and glared, “Eat a dick, Beverly!” She then slammed the front door, and Sondra and the other ladies walked toward the elevator. Sondra looked at Roxie and Lacy, “The nerve of that woman trying to tell everyone who they can and can’t pursue. She is the Bitch of all Bitches!”

Roxie nodded in agreement. Lacey replied, “You got that right!” The elevator arrived to take the ladies down to the first floor.

Beverly tried to compose herself. She turned her attention toward those that stayed, “Ladies, I’m so sorry for that outburst from Sondra . She must have forgotten to take her medication today.” There were nods and a few smiles. The ladies whispered among themselves." I don't have an excuse for Roxanne or Lacey . They have always been followers. It looks like we need a new secretary since Roxanne has left our club . Do I have any volunteers?" Beverly looked around the room . No one raised their hand, "Okay, then it looks like I will have to appoint one of you. I will make that announcement at our next meeting; it will be held at Vera Park's apartment. Unless any of you have questions." The room was quiet. "What? No questions? Then let's enjoy our wine and time together." Beverly put on her best fake smile, trying to hide her anger as she poured herself another glass of wine. The rest of the 'Sunset Sisters' gathered around the counter as wine was filling up empty glasses.

Those that remained in Beverly's apartment after her outburst tried to enjoy themselves. They knew how controlling Beverly was. You never wanted to get on her bad side. It was best to stay quiet and out of her view . She would calm down eventually.

Hazel, who was petite with short white hair, asked Edna, "What happened to Beverly's husband?" Edna took a sip of her rose' wine and replied, "He died." Hazel whispered back to Edna, "Was it natural or by choice?" Edna tried not to choke on her wine from laughter, "If I was married to her, I would have died by choice." Both women started to giggle.

Hazel and Edna were sisters . Actually, they were stepsisters. Edna's father married Hazel's mother. They had grown up together in a religious home, Edna's father was a deacon at church, and Hazel's mother taught the youth group. Dancing and makeup were a big 'no, no' according to their father. The girls grew up and attended a Christian college. They entered the workforce; Hazel was a secretary for a big accounting corporation, while Edna was hired as a paralegal for a criminal attorney. The sisters stepped away from their strict upbringing. Taking pride in their appearance, they wore makeup. Their faces were freshened up with pink blush, and their lips were coated with red lipstick. They dated but never married. They had been proposed to many times. They enjoyed dating, especially going out dancing. The sisters never understood why they couldn't dance when they were younger. Growing up watching their parents, marriage didn't appeal to them. They enjoyed the company of a man and had a few sexual encounters during their younger days. They never understood the big deal that was made about sex. They found it could be quite enjoyable. When the time came for them to retire, Hazel found Sunset Village in Summers Bay. They found it lovely and moved into one of the largest two-bedroom condos together.

Beverly held her wine glass up, "Ladies, I'd like to make a toast if I may." They all raised their glasses up. Beverly smiled, "May all your ups and downs be between the sheets . Cheers!"

"Cheers!" was said in unison, and laughter filled the small apartment.

***

Sondra's apartment

Roxanne and Lacey joined Sondra in her apartment to share a glass of wine. Sondra opened a bottle, "I hope you like Moscato . It's on the sweet side." Lacey held her glass out, "One of my favorites. Roxanne brushed a few strands of hair behind her ear, "I prefer a glass of sweet wine . I find dry wine is like drinking dust."

Lacey looked around Sondra's apartment, "Wow! Sondra, you really have a flair for décor." Sondra blushed, "Why thank you, I have always liked putting things together. It doesn't matter if it's furnishings, clothes, or accessories. I love to mix styles."

Lacey nodded her head toward Sondra's bedroom, "Do you mind if we take a peek around?" Sondra felt proud of the work she put into her apartment and was happy to show it off, "Come on, let me show you the bedroom and master bath." The ladies followed her into the bedroom. "If you look to your left, you will see my closet . I have it packed with shoes and clothes. I have this naughty little habit . It's called shopping." Sondra put her hand up to her mouth and giggled.

Roxie and Lacey giggled along with her. “That we understand,” Roxie replied.

Sondra opened her closet bifold doors. She pulled a string that turned on a light inside the closet. Both women “Oohed” and “Awed” as they looked at the racks of shoes on top and bottom of the closet, under the hanging clothes. The clothes were put in order according to height and color. Lacey let out a little cry, “Oh my god, I think I just had an orgasm!” Roxanne picked up a pair of black satin heels that had rhinestones around the back of the heel, “Oh my, these are beautiful!” She looked inside the shoe, “Sondra, we wear the same size!” She said with excitement, “Can I try them on?” Sondra giggled, “Of course, you can.” Roxie slipped out of her shoes and into the satin heels, “Fits like a glove,” she walked over to the full-length mirror on the wall to see how they looked on her feet. Sondra sipped her wine as she watched Roxie walk in front of the mirror, admiring the shoes, “You’re welcome to borrow them.” Roxie turned toward Sondra, “Really? I would love to take them for a spin.”

“Just don’t forget where you got them, you hear?” Sondra replied with a smile.

“Oh, I won’t . I promise to take very good care of them. “Roxie put her shoes back on, holding onto the black heels, “Do you have something I can put them in?” Sondra handed Roxie a box from the closet.

Sondra turned to the left, “I just had the master bath redone to my taste.” They followed Sondra to the bathroom door. The ladies walked in . There were more “oohs” and “Awes.”

Roxie looked the bathroom up and down, “I want one of these in my apartment. Sondra, this is absolutely beautiful!” Roxie walked over to the soaking tub, “I’m definitely getting myself one of these!” Lacey sipped her wine as she admired the tile work, “Sondra, you have a real eye for design.” Sondra shyly smiled, “Thank you. Roxie,

Lacey, let me fill your glasses up." The ladies walked back toward the kitchen.

The wine flowed until the bottles were emptied . They laughed, and shared stories about Beverly, how she tried to control everyone. They talked about what single men were available and how they might score a date with the man of their choice. All three agreed Beverly Johnson would not dictate who they could and could not pursue.

Beverly Johnson's apartment

As the wine bottles were emptied and the cheese disappeared, the ladies started to leave. Hugs and air kisses were exchanged.

Hazel and Edna were the last two to leave. You could always count on them to help clean up.

Beverly smiled, "Don't worry about the rest . I'll take care of it. You go and have your dinner."

Edna picked up a few more dishes and added them to the sink, "Can I use your restroom?"

"Of course, you know where it is."

Edna returned after a few minutes. The sisters picked up their purses, and Beverly walked them to the door. "Thanks, Beverly . We will see you around."

Beverly closed the front door, "I don't know why those two old crows keep coming to these meetings. I've never seen them with any man. Spinsters! If it hasn't happened by now, ladies, It never will." Beverly laughed out loud.

She started to clean up . She washed the wine glasses, trying to think of a way to get back at Sondra, Roxanne, and Lacey for causing her embarrassment. *The nerve of them! Attacking me in front of my club members!* She kept replaying the event in her head, how they stormed out during a meeting. She whispered to herself, "I swear you three will pay for your disrespect." She finished up in the kitchen and decided to go downstairs for dinner.

Beverly changed her clothes, touched up her makeup, and added a spritz of hairspray to her hair. She walked over to the closet door mirror. She made sure everything was in place. Playing with her hair, she said aloud, "I'm ready to make my entrance into the dining room." She left her apartment, taking the elevator down to the first floor.

***

Dining Room

Beverly knew how to make an entrance. As she entered the dining room, she noticed Fergus sitting by himself in a small round booth. He was looking at the menu and hadn't noticed Beverly as she slid into his booth. He lowered his menu and realized he had company.

"Good evening, Fergie . You don't mind if I call you Fergie, do you? I noticed you were all alone and thought I would join you for dinner. I hope that's okay with you."

Fergus swallowed as he put his menu down. He was surprised by his unexpected dinner companion. "Hello Beverly, to be honest with you, I was not expecting anyone to join me. I was planning on having a quiet dinner by myself."

"Oh, don't be silly . Nobody likes to eat alone. This will be a good way for us to get to know one another, don't you think?" Beverly scooted further into the booth and closer to Fergus, just enough to look like it was a dinner date.

Fergus, being at a loss for words at this intrusion, decided to make the best of it and plan better for next time.

"Beverly, I understand that you are a very friendly woman. However, I do like to eat alone . I've been doing it for years. I enjoy the solitude."

The waitress brought Beverly a dinner menu to the table, "I'll give you two a few minutes and be back for your order."

"Oh, come on, Fergie, you didn't move into this beautiful place to be alone. You and Brian have struck up a friendship. You can't have too many friends."

Beverly picked up the menu. "What are you going to have? I heard we have a new chef. I think I might try the lasagna. I hear it's to die for." Fergus, feeling trapped, replied, "You do that . I am going with the meatloaf."

Just then, the waitress returned to take their order. Beverly ordered a glass of wine to go with her dinner. Fergus asked for a refill of his water.

"Wonderful choices . I'll be back with your orders in a jiffy." The waitress took the menus and wandered to the next table.

Fergus wasn't big on small talk. Beverly continued to talk for them both. She would ask a question here and there and then would go back to talking about herself and the clubs she was involved in. Fergus listened without really listening . In other words, he tuned her out.

"Fergie, you should really think about joining a club."

Fergus grunted.

"It's a great way to get to know folks. We have a wonderful singles club I think you would enjoy."

"I'm not interested in clubs. I am just going to enjoy my retirement on my terms."

Just then, the waitress returned with their dinner choices. As she sat them down in front of them. Fergus thought, *thank God for small favors . Hopefully, she won't talk while she's eating.*

"Wow, this looks amazing. Could I get another glass of wine?" Beverly waved her empty wine glass.

Fergus was surprised at the meatloaf. It not only looked wonderful, but it also tasted wonderful. He was reminded of his grandmother's cooking, "This is very flavorful; I hope this new chef makes everything else taste this good."

"Oh, Fergie, I'm so glad you are enjoying your meal. Isn't this nice, just the two of us?"

Fergus muttered as he cut into his meatloaf. Beverly smiled at Fergus while tasting a bite of her lasagna. She knew he would enjoy dining with her.

The waitress arrived with Beverly's wine, "Is there anything else I can get for you two? Desert, maybe?"

Fergus shook his head no while he gave her a half smile.

Beverly picked up her wine glass as she gazed around the room. She hoped they would be noticed as a couple. She did catch the eyes of a few 'Sunset Sisters' who were also having dinner. Beverly smiled at them as she turned her gaze toward Fergus. He looked at her at the perfect time. They did look like a couple. She knew this would be tomorrow's gossip.

"Everything ok?" he asked.

Beverly's smile widened as she replied, "It couldn't be any better."

As the two finished up their meal. Fergus slid out of the booth, "I'm going to head back to my apartment."

"Wait, Fergie, I'll walk out with you."

Fergus stood up by the table . Beverly slid out on the same side . She stood beside Fergus and grabbed his arm as they walked toward the door. Just as they were walking out, Sondra, Lacey, and Roxanne were walking in. Beverly just smiled at them as she snuggled close to Fergus.

Hazel and Edna weren't far behind Beverly and Fergus. Edna nudged Hazel, " That woman works fast!" she whispered. Edna put her index finger up to her mouth, " Shh, we don't want them to hear us."

Fergus walked Beverly to the elevator, "I believe this is your stop."

"Would you like to come up? We could watch a movie together."

"I don't think so. You go ahead." He took her arm off his and walked down the hall toward his apartment.

Beverly called after him, "Next time?" She blew him a kiss as he walked away.

Fergus continued down the hall, not looking back.

Edna and Hazel took the next elevator behind Beverly up to the second floor. Hazel looked at Edna, and the sisters smiled at each other. They didn't have to talk . They knew what the other one was thinking.

Roxanne, Lacey, and Sondra found themselves an available table for dinner. The waitress brought them menus and gave them a few minutes to decide .

"Oh, my God! Did you see that?" Lacey shook her head as she looked at the menu.

Roxanne looked at Lacey, "You know he didn't ask her to dinner. I know her tactics . She doesn't fool me one bit!"

Sondra laughed, "You know she is trying to make a point; she's like a dog marking its territory. That is one crazy bitch if you ask me."

Roxanne and Lacey replied, "Yes!" in unison.

Roxanne set her menu down, "I hope Fergus knows what he has himself in for with that one." Lacey looked around the dining room, "Let's hope he can see right through her. With him being a retired detective, he must see what she is up to." The three friends ate dinner and parted ways afterward .

Chapter 6:
Trapped

Beverly walked into her apartment feeling excited. She kicked off her high heels and tossed her pocketbook onto a nearby chair. She had dinner with Fergus, and she was on cloud nine. *Timing couldn't have been any better,* she thought to herself.

She walked into her bedroom and opened a drawer where she kept her silky nightwear.

"This is what I'm looking for." She pulled out a white- slip nightie. She undressed and put it on. She checked herself out in a nearby mirror.

Fergus was relieved that dinner was over. He shook his head in disbelief and thought to himself, *Why do I attract women like Beverly?*

As he took off his jacket, he got a whiff of her perfume. He opened the patio door and hung it on a chair to air out.

Beverly fixed her lipstick. Her thoughts were working overtime; now she had to figure out how to get him up here. She poured herself a glass of wine, and sighed to herself. "Hmm."

She picked up the phone and called Fergus.

Fergus took his time to answer, "Hello."

"Fergus!" Beverly sounded out of breath.

"Yes, what can I do for you?"

"Fergus, it's me Beverly."

"Yes, I see that on my caller ID."

"Help!" she said, sounding out of breath, "Someone's in my apartment!"

The phone went dead, Fergus groaned as he put his shoes back on. He took his time as he walked toward the elevator.

Beverly smiled as she hung up and laid the phone down. With a wine glass in hand, she unlocked her front door leaving it ajar.

The hallway was quiet . People were still in the dining room. Fergus pushed the button for the elevator and the door opened. Just as he was getting into the elevator, Sondra, Roxie, and Lacey were coming out of the restaurant. Sondra was talking when Roxie touched her arm, "Do you see what I see?"

Sondra covered her mouth with her hand, "Oh my god!"

Lacey stopped dead in her tracks, "I'll bet he's on his way to that Venus Fly Snatches' apartment." She looked at Roxie and Sondra, "I wonder if she put something in his drink?"

Sondra laughed, " Like what, Love Potion No. 9?" They all started laughing.

Lacey, still staring at the elevator, said, "They did look cozy after dinner. Maybe he decided to go up for dessert."

They looked at each other in unison and said, "Nah!"

Fergus knocked on Beverly's door. It was ajar; he called out, "Beverly, where are you?"

Beverly heard Fergus come in, that is when she let out a blood-curdling scream.

Fergus rushed into the bedroom to see her up against the wall. She looked shaken and pointed toward the bed. Fergus motioned for Beverly to move toward the bathroom. In a loud and assertive voice, he called out, "COME OUT FROM UNDER THERE ; IT'S OVER." There was no movement from under the bed.

Beverly slowly moved toward the bedroom door, closed and locked it. Fergus got down on his knees, he looked under the bed, then stood up. He looked at Beverly, "There is no one there, but you already knew that, didn't you?"

"They must have heard me when I called you and left. I was in the bathroom getting ready for bed."

"Yes, I can see that. Are you expecting company?"

Beverly smoothed her nightgown with her hands moving them slowly down the curves of her body, "No, just you." She said in a sultry tone.

Fergus walked up to her; she looked shapely in her nightgown. He started to feel something he hadn't felt in a while. Trying to control his urges he reached for the doorknob, she moved closer to him, she pressed her body up against his.

"Oh my, Fergie, did you bring your gun?" She licked her lips.

She put her left hand on his chest as she grinded her hips against him. She slowly reached down with her right hand; he was ready for her. She unzipped his pants, she sighed, as she reached her hand inside, "Oh my, is that for me?" she asked in a sultry whisper as she looked up into his eyes.

Fergus, feeling trapped, made a decision, knowing it wasn't a good one. He picked her up, carried her to the bed and gently laid her down. She pulled him close to her . He leaned in and they kissed for the first time. It was passionate; their hearts beat in rhythm, their breathing picked up. He cupped her face with his hands, " You planned this, didn't you?"

She smiled, " And if I did?"

His hands still cupping her face, " Then you're a naughty girl."

Beverly smiled, "Maybe you should spank me." Fergus smiled, "Maybe I should." They kissed again.

Beverly reached to unbutton his shirt. Fergus removed his clothing; he watched as she slowly removed her nightgown and kicked off her lace panties. There was something about her, she was like a magnet he couldn't get away from. He knew this might come back to haunt him, but his emotions took over. He was no longer thinking with his head. Beverly moaned softly as Fergus made love to her. Their bodies entangled within the sheets. When she had reached that moment of ecstasy, she called out," "Ah" that was wonderful" as her body relaxed. "Fergie, this was even better than I had imagined." She cuddled close to him. She smiled and they kissed once more. He sat up. She reached for his arm, "Don't leave not yet, stay for a bit." He leaned toward her and gently kissed her forehead. She reached for him as he stood up.

He dressed himself, "I'll let myself out." He walked toward the bedroom door.

She grinned ear to ear, "Until next time?"

Fergus turned toward her and smiled, "We'll see." She heard him lock the door as he left.

He walked toward the elevator talking to himself, "What did I just do? She planned this, and it worked. Beverly, you are a vixen!"

Beverly rolled up in the bedsheet, and she hugged herself, she felt like she had just won the lottery, "He's mine!", she whispered to herself, "He's all mine."

Fergus back in his apartment jumped into the shower, replaying the evening in his head. Wondering how he could let this happen?

Sondra's apartment

Sondra arrived back at her apartment after dinner. She decided to put on her comfy lounge pants and t-shirt. Her favorite television show would be starting soon. She cuddled up on the couch with a blanket her mother had crocheted for her years ago, when the phone rang.

"Hello?" she could hear breathing.

"Hello, who is this?" Still no answer, just breathing.

"Beverly is that you?" Click. Sondra hung up the phone, "That woman! I know that was you, Bev."

Sondra turned the television to her show. Afterwards She folded her blanket and laid it over the back of the couch. Yawning, she decided to call it a night. The phone rang again. She looked at the clock, "Who is calling me at eleven pm?" She picked up the phone.

"Hello?" the line was open, she could hear breathing, "Who is this? Beverly?" Click.

She hung up the phone. "Beverly, you will be hearing from me in the morning!"

Turning off the lights, Sondra turned in for the night. She laid in bed tossing and turning until she fell asleep.

The morning sun was rising, spring was turning to summer. Light peeked through the bedroom curtains waking her up. She sat up in bed still tired from the night before. She yawned as she slipped into her slippers.

Shuffling toward the kitchen for a cup of coffee. There was a knock at the door. Looking up at the clock on the wall, she walked toward the door.

"Who is it?" still trying to wake up.

"It's me Roxie, let me in."

Sondra opened the door; Roxie was wearing her exercise clothing.

"I thought you would be ready for our Zumba class this morning."

"Oh, I forgot. Do we have time for a quick cup of coffee?"

"Always, Roxie smiled."

"Good, you fix the coffee while I change."

Sondra quickly changed into her workout attire. She called out to Roxie from the bedroom, "I wonder if Beverley will show up."

"She always does, I'm sure she will want to gloat after we saw her with Fergus last night."

Sondra walked into the kitchen just in time to grab her cup of coffee.

"I'm sure it was her calling me last night and hanging up. All I could hear was breathing. I know it was her."

Roxie sipped her coffee "I wonder why she would do that?"

"Who knows that woman has a screw loose somewhere in that crazy brain of hers."

The ladies finished their coffee and were out the door in no time.

The following morning

In the dining room Fergus met up with Brian, the waitress had just brought them their coffee.

"What's new with you?" Brian asked.

"That's a question I really don't want to answer. If I don't answer, you'll hear about it through the gossip that goes on in this place."

"I'm intrigued, spill it."

"Last night all I wanted was to have a quiet dinner alone, Beverly showed up and joined my table."

"Of course, she did." Brian laughed.

"That's not all."

Brian sipped his coffee, "Don't tell me, let me guess. Knowing what I know about her she hooked you in didn't she?"

"In a manner of speaking you could say that."

"That woman has a way of getting what she wants."

"I agree with you on that. She claimed there was an intruder in her apartment, of course there wasn't."

"I'm getting the picture; she is a sly one."

"Now I'm afraid it's going to get weird. I've got to let her know that was a one time thing."

"Ah, she isn't going to like that."

"Maybe not, I will not get into another relationship with a woman like her. She is reminiscent of my last wife. Let me tell you that one was a shark!"

"I wish you good luck my friend. Don't look now but she just came through the door."

Beverly was all smiles as she entered the dining room, she waved at Brian and Fergus. She walked up to their table, "Good morning fellows, mind if I join you?" She slid in next to Fergus. He grumbles as he moves over for her.

"I see you haven't had that first cup of coffee yet Fergie, a little grumpy in the morning, are you?"

Fergus shook his head no, "I was hoping to have a quiet breakfast with my friend Brian here."

"Oh, I don't mean to intrude. I'll leave you to it then." She got up and went over to join another table.

Brian looked surprised, "Wow, that was easy. She seemed to be in a good mood. Maybe your visit with her last night is what she needed. You fixed her." Brian laughed. Fergus didn't find Brian's humor funny this time.

"I didn't visit her, she tricked me into coming up to her apartment."

"Well, it worked. That one can be a bit bitchy. All I'm saying is she is very pleasant this morning."

Beverly sat with Edna and Hazel ladies from her 'Sunset Sisters' Club. They were all smiles as they listened to her telling them who knows what. They did look over at Brian and Fergus a couple of times and smiled.

The men finished their breakfast. They went off in different directions. Fergus back in his apartment decided to go fishing, he needed to get out for a while.

Out on the pier he caught and released several fish. It felt good to be out with the ocean air in his face. Fishing always took his mind off whatever was bothering him. After a couple of hours, he headed back, taking his time.

Back in his apartment the phone rang, "Hello."

"Fergie, is that you? I thought I'd wait awhile before I called. I wanted to make sure you were settled in before I bothered you."

"Lily?" he said with a smile in his voice.

"Yes, how are you?"

"It's nice to hear from you."

"Well, tell me about your place and the people you've met. I can't wait to hear all about it."

"There is so much to tell. I have an idea; why don't you drive over when you have some time off. I'd love to show you around. They have guest quarters here, it's like a motel room. Let me know and I'll book you a room."

"Sounds fun! It just so happens I have the next two days off. If you can't book a room this late, I can find a motel, I'm sure."

"Wonderful, I'll see you when you get here. Bring some clothes for the pool and fishing."

"You got it." Fergus was excited that his partner from Springfield Police Department would be visiting.

Chapter 7:
Medical Examiner's Office

Results had come back from the lab on Blanche Smith. Doc Thompson was going over the results while he tapped his pencil on his desk. "Hum, hum" he said again and again.

Kelly walked over to see what was so interesting, "Well, what does it say? I'm on pins and needles here."

"I'm going to call Darcy Smith and tell her the results of the autopsy." Kelly crossed her arms, "Do I get to find out before she does?" Doc Thompson handed the results to Kelly, "I don't understand, it says her cause of death is due to natural causes. What is natural about a dildo being pushed into her throat?"

Doc Thompson scratched his head with his pencil, "Blanche had a fatal amount of adrenaline in her system which caused her to have a heart attack." Kelly looked puzzled, "What does that mean?" She hands the results back to Eric.

"It means there was something that caused adrenaline to be released. Fear, panic, a strong emotional reaction. Something or someone caused increased levels of adrenaline that shot through her body's system reaching her heart causing a fatal heart attack. You're familiar with the saying "scared to death?"

Kelly was surprised at what Doc was saying, "Yes, I've heard of that before. I always thought that was just a saying and not something that could really happen."

"A terrifying event can cause this. It can happen to anyone; it causes a fight or flight response."

Kelly looked surprised at what she heard, "Wow! That is the craziest thing I've ever heard. If someone scared this woman to death wouldn't that be a crime?"

"I'm not sure. Our sheriff won't be looking into it that I'm sure of."

Kelly sat down at her desk, "Especially when the cause of death is listed as natural. I don't see how being scared is a natural way to die."

"It's listed as natural due to her having a heart attack. When we watch a scary movie, we have a release of adrenaline in our system because it's scary, something you are not expecting happens. When you walk alone at night to your car in a dark garage or parking lot your body can release adrenaline due to you being afraid something might happen. When the body responds to a sudden scare, stress or something dangerous, extra adrenaline is pumped throughout your system. Your brain is telling you to run or react to the situation at hand. It's actually very rare that someone is scared to death. Age and heart condition can be a factor."

Kelly is still trying to understand what she just heard, "The one thing I do know is our bumbling sheriff is wrong. This death is definitely not a suicide."

"That we know is true."

Doc sat at his desk with the results in hand, he made the phone call to Darcy Smith. He filled her in on what the results were. She took it well and is making plans to have her aunt's body transferred to Springfield.

Now shall we get ready for our next customer?" Eric laughed.

"You know I hate it when you talk that way, Eric."

"Yes, I know that is why you are so fun to tease. We do need to file these reports. Why don't you take the rest of the day off? I'll call you if I need you to come back in. Go do something fun."

"Thanks, I'll do just that."

Kelly straightened up her desk, "I'll see you tomorrow unless I hear from you sooner."

Doc waved as she exited.

Chapter 8:
Shades of Green

Lily arrived in Summers Bay just after four in the afternoon. She made a stop at a supermarket to pick up a few things, she noticed there was a plant section and decided to bring Fergie a housewarming gift. She picked out a snake plant. *Fergie can't kill this even if he tried.* She thought to herself. Water every two weeks and it will grow.

She parked her car in the guest parking area. Lily walked into Sunshine Village and was surprised to see how beautiful the lobby area was. She was met by a woman at a counter, "Can I help you?"

"Yes, I'm here as a guest of Fergus Quimby. He is expecting me."

The lady at the counter called Fergus to let him know his guest had arrived. Fergus arrived in the lobby in no time to greet Lily.

"Fergie," Lily called out with excitement. The two hugged.

"This is my guest Lily Bright; I have a reservation for her in the guest quarters."

The counter lady checked her computer and handed Fergus the key.

"You made good time, are you hungry?"

Lily pushed a few strands of hair behind her ear, "Famished!" she smiled.

"Good! Let's get you to your room, then I'll take you to dinner."

Lily's guest room

"Fergie, this is beautiful! I might never leave." She looked around while Fergus sat her suitcase on the bed.

"I brought you a little housewarming gift." She handed him the plant she picked out for him. "I can't wait to see your apartment. I'd like to freshen up before we go to dinner."

Fergus looked at the plant wondering what he was going to do with it, "Let me take this back to my apartment and I'll come back in twenty minutes. Will that give you enough time to freshen up?"

"Yes, I'll see you then." Fergus let himself out.

Dining room

Fergus and Lily entered the dining room, they found a booth in the back where they could eat and visit without being disturbed. Lily was tall with shoulder length dark brown hair she was wearing black slacks with a cold-shoulder dark blue blouse. No sooner had they sat down when Beverly walked in.

Beverly dressed to the nines in hopes of having dinner with Fergus again, she noticed he was seated in the back with a woman she had not seen before. If looks could kill, she was shooting darts at this woman.

Lily noticed Beverly right away, "Fergie, who is that woman staring at us?"

"Her name is Beverly; she has this idea that we have a thing going on."

Lily started to giggle, she put her hand up to her mouth trying not to be obvious.

"Fergie, I need to hear this story." She whispered.

The waitress showed up bringing them their menus and water.

Beverly sat alone at a table facing in the direction of Fergus and Lily's booth. She could feel the heat rising in her face.

Lily was right, if looks could kill, she would have evaporated.

Fergus found the situation a bit comical. He looked at the menu trying not to look at Beverly. "Do you see anything that you might like?" setting his menu down.

"Lily still checking out her choices, "Yes, there are a couple of things that look good. I'm still trying to figure out which one I want."

"The food is good; I can tell you I haven't had a bad meal here yet. Make sure you save room for dessert."

"I'll try." She said with a smile.

Beverly sat quietly with a glass of white wine, staring at Fergus off and on. She thought she could feel her blood boiling. Who is that woman? She's young enough to be his daughter. Her thoughts were spinning while she sipped her wine, so much so she didn't notice Sondra take a seat at her table.

"Well, well, well, looks like Fergus found himself a sugar baby," she said with a laugh. She waved at the waitress for a glass of wine and a menu.

"I hope you don't mind that I joined you, you looked lonely, and I just can't stand that look on you."

Beverly looked Sondra square in the face giving her a forced smile. “Sondra, I’d be very careful if I were you.” Sondra knew she had hit a nerve.

“Come on Bev, lighten up.” She smiled back at her.

Beverly gritted her teeth together, raising her voice. Diners at nearby tables heard her as she said. “Don’t make me hunt you down. You know I’ll make it look like an accident, so don’t push me!”

“Oh, stop it, you’re scaring me.” She said with a laugh. “Did your little plan to hop on pop, not work out for you last night?” Sondra started to laugh out loud. The waitress set down her wine. Sondra held up her glass to Bev, “Here’s to better luck next time. You might have better luck with Eugene look, he’s watching you.”

“Shut up Sondra! I’ve warned you.” Beverly’s face was red, and she had fire in her eyes.

Sondra continued to laugh at her. That was the one thing that infuriated her more than anything, being made fun of. She could dish it out, she just couldn’t take it. Sondra was the only one who ever stood up to her, she knew the buttons to push.

She knew she had her right where she wanted. Sondra challenged Beverly, “Make me, bitch!” she said with a raised voice.

Lily and Fergus couldn’t help but overhear the confrontation going on between the two women. Their voices carried in the large dining room. Other diners were watching as well. Eugene sat in his usual seat at the back of the room facing the entrance, eating his meal in silence as he always does. Watching with interest.

Sondra and Beverly ordered their dinner. The two continued their banter during dinner. Sondra accused Beverly of calling her and hanging up. “I’ve done no such thing! Why on earth would I do that? Believe me when I say, you are just not that interesting.”

Fergus and Lily enjoyed their meal along with dessert. They laughed as they reminisced over their last case together. Lily filled Fergus in on the local happenings in Springfield since he retired. It was fun to catch up with each other.

There was a loud scream, "ARE YOU CRAZY?" Sondra stood up; she was wet from the water that Beverly had just thrown on her.

"Dinner and a show, how thoughtful of you Fergie."

Fergus laughed, "I've missed your humor Lil."

Trying to ignore what was going on, Lily and Fergus carried on with their conversation.

"So, what do you have planned for us these next couple of days?"

"I'll give you a tour of this place, we can go out to the pool and later I'm going to take you fishing."

"Oh, goody I can't wait."

Sondra wiped the water off her face with a napkin then threw it at Beverly. She stormed out of the dining room while Beverly sat and continued to stare at Fergus and Lily. Eugene finished his meal; he stopped at Beverly's table and shook his head in disbelief. Beverly stared back at him, "What are you looking at? Mind your own damn business, will you?" Eugene continued toward the door.

"Lil, let's go to my apartment. Things will be quieter there." The two headed toward the door, they were followed by Beverly. She watched them walk down the hall. Fergus noticed her as they entered his apartment.

Sondra's apartment #114

Sondra removed her wet blouse, "That bitch!" she said out loud, "I'll get back at you for this." She walked over to her closet looking for a change of clothes.

The telephone rings, "Hello." No answer.

"Hello, I know it's you Bev. What do you want?" Still no answer. She hung up the phone. I swear that woman needs mental health therapy, maybe shock treatments will help her. The thought of Beverly lying still for shock therapy made her laugh, "Give that woman a lobotomy while you're at it" she laughed.

She walked back over to her closet, picked out a change of clothes and a pair of heels to match. She thought she heard something in the other room, "Is somebody there?" no answer, it's probably nothing, noises carry around this place. After she changed her clothes, she picked up her wet blouse and laid it on the bed. She sat on the edge of the bed when she was hit from behind. Trying to see who was there, she stumbled to the floor. Laying in front of the closet door trying to sit up, "YOU!" she screamed when she was hit in the face. Her head fell back onto the floor with a thud.

Wine time at the Bistro

Roxie and Lacey met up in the Bistro for a glass of wine. The ladies had been busy with their usual activities throughout the day, "Where's Sondra?" Lacey asked.

"She should be here shortly; you know when we tell her a time, she always shows up thirty minutes late."

"I think we need to tell her thirty minutes earlier than we want to meet so she will show up on time." Roxie laughed, "That might work, let's do that next time."

The ladies shared small talk while they waited for Sondra. They decided to order a glass of wine.

"Sondra can catch up with us when she gets here." Lacey said, while she looked over the wine list.

Roxie and Lacy sat at a high top in the Bistro sipping their wine while they people watched. There are 200 apartments at Sunshine Village. They were almost at capacity, which made people watching fun. They noticed a few new faces and wondered if any more single men might have moved in.

Roxie kicked Lacey under the table as a salt and peppered-haired, tall distinguished looking man walked toward their table. "Hello, ladies," he said in a flirty voice. Lacey smiled; Roxie took a sip of her wine, "Well hello, are you lost? We've never seen you before."

"No, I'm not lost. I bought an apartment here a couple of months ago. I just moved in two days ago."

"That's nice, how does your wife like it here?" Lacey asked with a smile.

"Oh, I'm not married. Do you know what my shirt is made of?"

Both ladies looked at each other and smiled, then at this handsome man.

"No, enlighten us." Roxie shyly said.

"Boyfriend material. Hey, I'm just joking with you, I've never married."

"Really? Why is that?" Lacey sipped her wine.

"I guess I never found the right one."

Lacey was interested, "I like your sense of humor."

"What did you say your name was? I'm Lacey and this is my friend Roxie."

"I'm Doug Howard, nice to meet you two."

Roxie looked at the clock behind the counter, "We're waiting for a friend, or we would ask you to join us. It's not like Sondra to be this late, she knew we were meeting up here, didn't she?"

"Yes, I talked to her earlier and reminded her. She told me she never had to be reminded for wine thirty."

"It was a pleasure to meet you two ladies, I'm sure we will run into each other again," Doug said with a smile.

"Yes, we will be seeing you." Roxie said as she licked her lips before she took a sip of her wine.

Roxie nudged Lacey, "He sure looks fine walking away." Lacey smiled, "He looks good coming or going."

"Sondra should have been here by now. Let's finish up and go find her."

Sondra's apartment

The ladies finished their wine. The two of them walked down the hall toward Sondra's apartment. The door was slightly open.

"SONDRA?" Lacey called out, "ARE YOU BACK THERE?"

"Let's go in" Roxie opened the door, "SONDRA?" There was no answer. The light was on in the bedroom. The ladies walked in and could see Sondra's feet by the closet door she had one high heel on. Roxie gasped as she got closer, she let out a scream. Lacey moved closer behind Roxie and saw Sondra on the floor, her eyes wide open, the matching high heel was shoved into her eye socket. Blood trickled down from her eye. Both women screamed.

"Oh my God, what do we do?" Roxie cried as she moved backward toward the door.

"We have to tell someone, but who?"

"What about Fergus? He was a detective and he would know what to do."

The ladies rushed out of Sondra's apartment and headed toward apartment 110. They walked as fast as they could in their high heels. It wasn't but a few doors down.

Roxie pounded with her fists on the door. Both ladies were in tears. Lily stood up wondering what was going on now. Fergus answered the door.

"Help! You've got to help! Someone killed Sondra." Roxie was at the point of hyperventilating.

"Where?" Fergus asked, sounding concerned.

"In her apartment she's dead by her closet, she was late meeting us, so we went to look for her. You've got to help!"

"Take us there, come on Lily." Lily followed; she grabbed her phone.

The two detectives followed Roxie and Lacey to Sondra's apartment.

"I'm going to have to ask you two to stay outside, don't go too far. I'm going to have a few questions for you."

Roxie and Lacey stood outside the apartment holding onto each other with tears in their eyes.

Lily walked over to the body, "This is the woman who was in the confrontation with your stalker."

"Yes, I can see that. There doesn't seem to be any sign of a struggle."

"Fergie, I heard that Beverly woman threaten this one from our booth."

"Yes, I heard her too." He said in a flat tone.

"Well, do you think she could have done this?"

"It's hard to say, I know she can be sharp with her tongue. I don't picture her doing this."

"She got a bit nasty with her water glass. I wouldn't rule her out."

Lily made the call to the local sheriff's office. "He said he will be here as soon as he can. He asked me if I was sure she was dead. Then he told me she wasn't going to go anywhere."

"Wonderful, I've heard he is slow to move. With this being a small seaside town, I hear he does things on his own time."

"Well, I'm not going to sit and wait for him, I'm going to have a look around." Lily walked toward the front door, "Ladies how did you get in here?" Lacey walked up to Lily, "The door was slightly open. We called out for her. There was no answer, so we went in."

"Did you touch anything?"

They both shook their heads no, "No, just the door."

Lily walked to the patio door and noticed it was open as well. She looked in the kitchen, which appeared to be neat, nothing unusual.

Fergus walked into the bathroom, "Wow, this is way nicer than mine." Lily walked back to peek, "Very neat and clean, the only thing I noticed that was out of place was the wet blouse she was wearing earlier on the bed."

Sheriff Sam arrived, Fergus introduced himself and Lily. The sheriff walked over to the body and looked around, "I called the M.E. before I left the office. They should be here soon." The sheriff bent down and looked at Sondra, he then looked up into her closet at all the shoes. "Hmm" Fergus and Lily stood back to watch what he was doing.

The M.E. arrived with his assistant Kelly, they put the body in a black bag. The sheriff shook his head at the M.E., "looks like we have nothing more here than a household accident."

The M.E. looked at the sheriff, "So, we have death by stiletto sheriff, is that right?"

"Yep, if you noticed she is wearing one shoe. By my observation she was reaching for the other shoe then, bam! Right in the eye. It is a fact that most accidents happen at home. Case closed."

Kelly and Doc Thompson lifted the bag onto a gurney. Kelly was about to respond to what the sheriff had just said, Doc motioned for Kelly not to say anything.

Lily introduced herself to the M.E. and Kelly, "Here is my card, please give me a call when you have time." He nodded, as they rolled Sondra out toward the main entrance.

Residents crowded the hallway trying to find out what happened. Sheriff Sam assured them it was nothing more than an accident and they had to move along.

Fergus walked over to the closet, "Lily, come here and take a look at this."

Lily walked over, "Wow! This woman knew how to dress. Check out those red bottom shoes, this is a woman's dream."

"You're about the same height as Sondra was, see if you can reach the shoes easily."

Lily stood in front of the bifold doors and reached for a pair of shoes, "Not a problem, I don't have to stand on my toes to reach them." Lily grabbed one shoe and dropped it to the floor, it landed on its side. She did this a couple more times with the same results.

"There is no way a shoe fell from that shelf into her eye. If she was standing reaching for the shoe, it would have fallen onto the floor landing on its side not in her eye socket with the heel buried in her face. That stiletto made it to her eye with force."

"That's what I thought, there is more going on here than the eye can see, no pun intended." Fergus cracked a half smile.

"Where's your notebook? You should be taking this down."

"It's retired, like I am. And this is out of your jurisdiction."

"Maybe so, I'm still going to investigate. Are you with me?"

Fergus rubbed his chin, "I'm in." Fergus pulled out two pairs of gloves from his pocket, handing a pair to Lily.

"Good!" Lily replied.

Sheriff Sam walked back into the apartment, "Well, it was nice to meet you folks. Looks like I'm done here." He walked out toward Roxie and Lacey, "Ladies, sorry about your friend." Lacy and Roxie were still holding onto each other with tears in their eyes.

Fergus and Lily looked around the bedroom, under the bed and over toward the window.

Lily walked over to the dresser, she picked up a medium size trophy that laid on its side," Hey Fergie, get a load of this."

Fergus looked in her direction, "What is it?"

"A pageant trophy for Ms. Congeniality." Holding it up she laughed, "Sondra was in a senior pageant a few years back."

"Was it Springfield's pageant?"

"No, this is from the state pageant. I'm going to bag this; it could be a clue."

"Fergie, we need a forensics team."

"That would be us. I wonder where she would keep a flashlight."

Lily pulled her phone out of her pocket, she held her phone close to her face and said, "Lumos" the phone turned into a flashlight, "Here use this" and handed it to Fergus,

"Thanks, this is nice. I wonder if my phone has one of these."

"Fergie, you have an old flip phone, they don't come with one."

"I like my old flip phone; it does what I want it to."

Fergus shined the light under the bed, on the bed, around the bed and over in front of the closet.

"Do you see anything?" Lily asked.

"Maybe, see if you can find some tape and a couple of plastic bags."

Lily went into the kitchen opening drawers, "I've found plastic bags, give me a minute on the tape." She called out.

Roxie and Lacey stood in the front doorway. Lily looked toward them, "Do you know where I might find some tape?"

Roxie stepped inside the doorway, "Check in the bathroom, I believe Sondra has some in there, its garment tape but should work for you."

Lily brought the tape and bags to Fergus. Lily placed the trophy in a gallon bag. He picked up a couple of things with the tape and put them in the bags.

"What did you find?"

"Sondra has red hair; I've found a few strands of white hair, a button that doesn't match the blouse on the bed, there is a small amount of soil and wood shavings."

"Good job, we have clues." Lily smiled as Fergus handed her the bags.

"It's not much, it could be something, or it could be nothing at all. It was in front of the bed by the closet, that is where Sondra was found."

Lily took another look around, "Nothing else seems out of place. If there had been a robbery, there would be signs pointing to that. I believe she knew whoever was here. This was no accident. The only person that sheriff is fooling is himself."

Fergus handed the phone back to Lily. She held it up to her face and said," Nox" the light turned off, Fergus watched. He was fascinated, "What language does your phone speak?" Lily smiled, "It's not a language, it's a command to turn on and off the flashlight."

"Are you sure my phone doesn't have one of those?"

"I'm sure Fergie."

They walked toward the front door. Roxie and Lacey looked at them, "That was no accident," Roxie said with tears in her eyes.

Lily patted her shoulder, "We know, was there anyone that Sondra was having trouble with, a man or woman?"

Lacey wiped a tear from her eye, "Yes, Beverly! That bitch is evil."

"Anyone else?" Fergus asked.

"Sondra was a pretty lady, she had money. Look at her apartment, it's beautiful. I'm sure there are a few that were envious of her. Beverly didn't like her because she stood up to her. She wouldn't take any of her shit."

"Okay ladies, we may want to chat with you again. Thanks for your help."

The former partners checked out the patio door, "Fergie, lookie here. I can't move the door, it seems to be off the track." Fergus takes a closer look; he tries to move the door. "This won't budge. I'd say this could be the entry point." Lily took a picture with her phone. She also noticed there was dirt on the patio with a few landscape wood chips. "This looks like what was in the bedroom that you collected, could it be the same thing? Taking more pictures, "The local sheriff didn't even take the time to check this door or look out onto the patio."

Fergus looked out the patio door checking for windchimes, there weren't any. "Let's get out of here, I think we have enough." He and Lily walked back down to his apartment. Once inside Lily sat up at the counter, "Fergie, I know you have beer in your refrigerator I would like one please."

"You and me both."

Fergus grabbed a couple of beers, "Let's go out to the patio."

The two sat as the sun was setting, taking in the evening's events. Lily looked at him, "Tell me what is it with you and Beverly? Are you having an affair with her?"

"No, it was a one-time thing. It wasn't planned, she just kept after me. Joined me for dinner without being invited. Called me and told me someone was in her apartment which wasn't true, then seduced me."

Lily laughed, "I'm sorry but that sounds crazy!"

"She is crazy, I don't want anything to do with her, never did."

"Now that you slept with her, she is even crazier. She might think you two are an item. From the looks she was giving in our direction at dinner, she is a very jealous person. You saw the way she was looking at us. If she did kill Sondra, I might be next on her list."

Lily sipped her beer, "What are your thoughts about her?"

"To be honest, I really don't know much about her. She seems to have a strong personality. The women that are involved in the same clubs, follow her around like she's the queen bee."

Lily held up her beer bottle, "Is there anymore? I'm gonna need another one when this one is finished."

"Yep, let me grab us a couple." He walked over to the refrigerator.

"Ah, thanks." Lily smiled as he handed her another beer. "If I had to guess what happened in that apartment, I'd say Sondra left the front door unlocked knowing she would be leaving to meet up with her friends, or someone had a key. I did notice the patio door was ajar when we came in, so entrance could have been made there. As we looked closer the door was off track. Whomever came in killed her, then left through the front door leaving it open. Sondra had changed her clothes to meet up with friends. She was putting her shoes on when she was surprised from behind. Maybe she was struck with her own trophy. She turned around and managed to pull a button off what they were wearing, maybe the hair was transferred in the scuffle. The perpetrator grabs her high heel and hits her in the face with it."

"Wow!" Fergus took a drink of his beer, "You really have this figured out."

"It's not rocket science; I've learned from the best, you taught me well."

Fergus smiled, "Lil, you are a natural. I think you might have something there. Let's say that's what happened. What's the motive?"

"That's what has me puzzled. If I had to guess, I'd say jealousy. The ladies did say some were envious of Sondra due to her having money. Did she have her eye on you? Maybe she did and Beverly wasn't going to stand for the competition. Think about it."

"Maybe." He rubbed his chin, "I get your thinking. I just can't say one way or the other. I do think she knew the perpetrator."

"Let's think outside the box, maybe it could be someone else. Someone who you wouldn't suspect."

"That's always a possibility. The way that stiletto was planted in her face it would have to be someone that had the strength to do that."

"Beverly looks fit, she has a great shape and her body is toned. Do you know if she lifts weights or goes to the gym? You do have a gym here, don't you?"

"Yes, we have a nice gym with weights and workout equipment."

"Do you have a schedule of the happenings around here? Classes?"

"Yes, let me grab it."

Fergus retrieved the schedule for the month.

"This reminds me of a cruise ship's daily schedule. Wow, you have all kinds of things going on here from classes to entertainment. There happens to be a Zumba class in the morning, let's check it out and see who attends."

"I am not going to a Zumba or whatever class that is."

"No silly, we'll wait until after it starts then go down and see who is taking the class."

"Ok, afterward we'll go to breakfast. Tomorrow, I'll give you a tour then we'll spend some time by the pool. You're supposed to be taking time off."

Lily and Fergus chatted for the next hour, while they finished their beer.

"I'm going to head back to my room, I have to say this has been an interesting day."

"I'll walk you to your room and pick you up in the morning."

"It's a date, she said with a smile."

Chapter 9:
You Flipped The Bitch Switch, So Buckle Up!

The following morning Fergus arrived at Lily's room with coffee in hand. Lily opened the door.

"Fergie, my hero. You knew that was what I needed first thing." She said with a smile.

"Let me put on my shoes and I'm ready to see who shows up for that class."

The two walked the halls to the gym. Class had already started, there was a window where you could see the happenings inside. There were about fifteen women in class not counting the instructor and two men. The music was modern rock, and the movements were fast. No one noticed them watching.

"Look, there's your girlfriend in the back by the outside window."

Fergus laughed at that comment, "You mean my stalker."

"Yeah, whatever." She said with a giggle, "She has the moves down, look at her go!"

The two took notice of the others that were in the class including Roxie and Lacey. Beverly glanced toward the hall when the music changed; she noticed the class was being watched.

Fergus touched Lily's arm, "Let's go to breakfast, we've been seen."

"Let's come back later and see who uses the weight room."

The dining room was busy. Brian noticed Fergus and waved him over to his booth. Introductions were made. Brian asked questions about Sondra and the conclusions the sheriff came up with. The three enjoyed breakfast while brainstorming. Lily noticed the same man sitting in the back by himself.

"What's the story with that one?" she nodded toward Eugene.

Brian looked toward him, "He's a loner, stays to himself. I've never seen much interaction with anyone."

"I find that unusual, especially living in a place like this. You would think one moves here to enjoy what is offered and to make new friends."

Fergus wiped his mouth with his napkin, "I've seen him in the library and at the pool. He acknowledges you if you wave or say something. He just doesn't go out of his way to strike up a conversation with anyone."

"You know Fergie, it's the quiet ones you have to watch out for." She said with a smile.

"Well Brian, we're going to head out to the pool for a while."

"That sounds like an idea, maybe I'll see you two out there later."

Edna and Hazel were walking down the hall when they noticed Beverly quickly walking the other way. "What is she up to now?"

Hazel let out a sigh, "I can tell you whatever it is, it's no good."

Lily, Fergus and Brian headed toward the door just as Beverly walked in. Fergus nodded and smiled at her. She gave an icy stare to the three of them. She brushed Brian's shoulder as she walked by.

Before they separated in the hall, Brian said, "The ice queen has arrived. Maybe I'll see you two later."

"Nice to meet you, Brian." Lily waved.

"Fergie, I'll meet you back at your place after I change."

"Ok, see you in a few."

Lily opened the door to her room to find a note that was put under her door. She picked it up. It read –

I don't know who you think you are. I'm giving you fair warning to back off. You don't belong here.

It wasn't signed. "This must be from Beverly". She laid the note down. "That woman is a piece of work! The sooner Fergie sets her straight on where he is with her the better."

Lily changed into her bathing suit she brought. She pulled her hair up into a ponytail; grabbed a towel, sunscreen and her sunglasses. Taking the note with her to show Fergus.

Fergus' apartment

Fergus handed the note back to Lily, "This could have been written by anyone with these block letters. I wouldn't put it past Beverly to write this. There just isn't any proof that she did."

"Fergie, you know deep down she wrote this don't you?"

"I know she's capable of writing it, I just don't have proof that she did. Believe me when I say, I know this type of woman, she is like my ex. Let's go out by the pool and relax, I've got beer in this cooler."

He held it up, grabbed his towel. They walked out the sliding door onto the patio and toward the pool.

There were two lounge chairs side by side. Lily laid her towel out, removed her cover up and handed the sunscreen to Fergus, "Can you rub some of this on my back?"

Fergus took the sunscreen and applied it to her back. "I'm ready to jump in."

"Go ahead, I'm going to sun for a little bit first." Lily lay back on her lounge chair.

It was a warm morning. Lily noticed Eugene sitting under an umbrella reading a book. His nose was covered with white sunscreen, he had on white socks and tennis shoes. He was wearing a swimsuit. Strange, maybe he just got here. She thought.

"Lily" Fergus called, "Come on in, the water is nice."

Lily walked toward the pool, she dipped her toe in, "It's a little cold."

"Oh, come on Lil, you'll get used to it once you get all the way in. It's nice."

Lily walked down the steps then dropped down with a quick plunge up to her neck. She let out a little squeal," Ok, I'm in." she said with a smile, "This does feel nice once you get used to it. You have the perfect apartment close to the pool. I might move here myself when I retire."

"I'm starting to get used to it here, I'm glad this worked out."

Lily laughed, "How could you not get used to it here, you live in a resort. I know I'll be back to visit you again soon."

Lily and Fergus noticed the pool gate opened; Beverly walked in. She found a lounge chair across the pool from where Fergus was set up. Lily looked at Fergus and rolled her eyes. Fergus laughed, "I've never seen that look on you before."

She started to laugh with him, "It's leftover from my teenage years". Beverly didn't look amused. She settled in on her lounge chair, she applied sunscreen to her arms and legs. Her cold stare could be felt through the sunglasses she had on.

Fergus motioned Lily to come close, "Let's not focus on you know who, let's just keep our eyes open and enjoy ourselves." Lily nodded in agreement, then she splashed Fergus. They continued to laugh and chat.

"Fergie, I'm ready for a refreshment. How about you?"

Beverly watched them carefully. She pushed her sunglasses down on her nose, she watched over the top as they emerged from the pool.

Fergus pulled two beers out from the cooler, he opened one and handed it to Lily. The sun felt good, and the beer was cold.

"Hey, I noticed that quiet man under an umbrella over there. Does he come out here often?"

"I've seen him out here a time or two. He stays to himself reading."

"Do you think we should try to chat him up later? He might know a few things. He seems to be a people watcher."

"We could. Let's play it by ear for now."

"When are we going to go fishing? You know I've never been."

"I thought we would go early in the morning; would you be up for that?"

"I'm looking forward to it. Are we going to eat what we catch? If we catch anything?"

"Absolutely!"

Beverly felt defeated as she watched Fergus and his female companion as they enjoyed themselves. She thought for sure she would be by his side, especially after their tryst. Her schemes have always worked out in the past. She sipped a wine cooler she had brought to the pool.

Fergus tried to ignore the chill that was sent his way, he decided this would be a good time to introduce himself and Lily to Eugene. He pulled a beer out of the cooler, motioning for Lil to follow him. They walked up to the table where he sat under the umbrella.

"Hi, I was wondering if we could chat with you for a while. I brought you a refreshment."

Eugene smiled as he reached for the beer, "Thanks, please sit down."

"I'm Fergus." Before he could finish, Eugene interrupted, "I know who you are and that you're a retired homicide detective." He tried to act casually wondering. *Why do they want to talk to me? Did they find my pen?*

"Yes, I forget how quickly word travels here. This is Lily, she and I worked homicide together in Springfield. Lily has that job all to herself now."

"Nice to meet you both. What can I do for you?"

Lily cleared her throat, "We know you were dining during the commotion that took place yesterday."

"Yes, I saw what took place. I try to keep to myself. My wife Joan and I moved here to enjoy retirement, she passed unexpectedly a few months after moving here."

"I'm so sorry, had she been ill?"

"No, she was the picture of health. This place was new when we moved in, not too many residents like now. The more it filled up, clubs started, there were more activities to do. My Joan said she felt like she was back in high school."

"Why's that?" Fergus asked.

Eugene nodded toward Beverly, "Because of women like her. My Joan couldn't fit in with them, they 'snubbed' her as Joan called it. She was made to feel unwelcome. Joan wasn't a fancy woman and by that, I mean she wasn't stuck on herself and how she looked." Eugene looked over toward Beverly, "Like that one over there is. Don't get me wrong, Joan was a solid woman, she dressed nice, she just didn't do the nails, makeup, and hair like the others."

Fergus took a drink of his beer, "I understand what you're saying. Tell me how your wife passed?"

Eugene's eyes welled up, "She was depressed. She so wanted to be a part of things here. Rejection killed her. She ended her life with sleeping pills, she left me a letter that I later found stating what I just told you. Those women are ruthless, especially that one. She is the poison in this place."

Lily looked at Eugene and she could see the disgust he felt, "We are so sorry for your loss."

"Yes, we are sorry to hear about your wife. I have noticed since I moved in that you stay pretty much to yourself."

"Yes, I like it that way. I like to keep an eye on things that go on around me. I'm not interested in clubs. I do go out to the woodworking shop occasionally. During warm weather you will see me out here by the pool. I've heard some of the things that people say about me, that I'm a loner. I've been called a watcher of things. I've heard it said that I don't like people. I really don't care what people say or think."

Lily touched her nose, "Tell me about the heavy sunscreen on your nose, I'm just curious."

"I've had some skin cancers and I'm just being cautious. The reason for the socks too. One can't be too careful, you know."

Lily and Fergus agreed with a nod as they stood up, "If you see or hear anything that might be of interest regarding the death of Sondra Miller last night would you let me know?"

Eugene stood up, "I can do that, thanks for the beer." He held it up as if to toast them. He was relieved after they walked away.

They walked back to their lounges. Fergus sat on his chair as Lily applied sunscreen to his back. "You know he's right; you can't be too careful out here in the sun."

Lily's phone rang, she wiped her hands on her towel, "Lily, here." There was a long pause, "Yes, I'll tell him. We can be there shortly."

"Who was that?"

"Eric Thompson, M.E. He would like us to come down to his office. He said he has something to show us."

Fergus picked up his towel and cooler. Lil grabbed her things. Beverly watched the two with interest as they went into his apartment.

"Fergie, I'm going to go shower and change. I'll meet you back here. I won't be long."

Eugene saw the quick exit and thought, *something's going on. I wonder if they are off to arrest someone.*

Chapter 10:
The Medical Examiner's Office

Fergus and Lily arrived at the M.E. 's Office with the baggies of evidence they collected at Sondra's apartment.

Doc Thompson worked out of a small office with his assistant. It was adequate for the size of the town.

Kelly greeted the detectives, "We're so glad you were able to make it down here."

Lily smiled as they shook hands, "Thanks for inviting us."

Doc Thompson was standing by a table where the body of Sondra Miller laid, she was covered with a white sheet. "Yes, thanks for coming. I have some interesting things to show you."

Fergus and Lily followed Kelly over to the table the body was on. Doc Thompson pulled the sheet back away from Sondra's face. He turned her head to expose where she had been hit with something heavy enough to indent her skull. "This was not a household accident." He said with disgust in his voice, "That sheriff should be fired."

Fergus and Lily took a closer look at the wound. Lily held up the bag that had the beauty pageant trophy, "Could this have caused that injury?"

Doc reached for the bagged trophy to get a closer look. "Maybe." With gloved hands he removed the trophy from the bag and held it up to the wound. "The corner seems to fit the point of impact. However, it didn't kill her, it just stunned her or could have knocked her out or off balance." He placed the trophy back into the plastic bag, "I'll send this to the lab with her shoe and see if they can get anything off of it."

Lily handed Doc the other bags that were collected at the scene, "You might want to have these checked out as well."

"While our sheriff is off somewhere getting a haircut, or whatever he does when he is supposed to be working. I thank you both for stepping in."

Fergus smiled with a nod, "Lily is the one who pushed forward on this, if she hadn't been here, I probably wouldn't have gotten involved. I've looked forward to my retirement. I would have hoped we had a sheriff around here who took his or her job seriously."

Lily put her hands on her hips as she looked at Doc Thompson, "Are you going to report back to the sheriff letting him know he has a homicide on his hands?"

"Absolutely, he's not going to like that his household accident isn't an accident. He will be forced to do something about it."

Kelly chuckled, "You mean he might have to actually work?"

"That is exactly what I mean." He pulled the sheet to cover Sondra's face. Kelly moved the gurney back toward the refrigeration unit.

The detectives said their goodbye's, "Let us know what you find out."

Doc Thompson nodded and said he would.

Fergus and Lily headed back toward his apartment, "How would you like to stop for pizza?" He looked at Lily as her grin widened, she nodded while saying, "Yes! I'm famished after being out in the sun. It will be nice to eat in peace."

"I spotted this place when I moved here. It looks like a mom and pop's place."

"How did you figure that out?" Lily said with a laugh.

"By the sign, Momma and Pop's Pizza?"

Fergus laughed, "That was my first clue."

Fergus parked his car in front, Lily looked in the mirror on the visor and touched up her lipstick. As they walked up to the front door the smell of fresh pizza was delightful. Inside was reminiscent of an old Italian restaurant, red and white checkered tablecloths and curtains, wine bottles with candles in the tops set on each table with colored wax that had dripped down the sides. Music played in the background with Dean Martin singing 'That's Amore.' Fergus pointed to a table by a window. Lily hung her purse on the chair. The aroma of garlic sauce and bread filled the air.

A round Italian woman with short dark curly hair handed them menus, "You two look hungry, everything is homemade. Can I get you something other than water?"

Lily smiled as she peeked at the menu, "I would love to have a glass of Lambrusco." Fergus raised his index finger, "Make that two please." The woman smiled at them, "Good choice, I'll be back in a minute to take your order."

Lily was taking in the atmosphere, "What a quaint place! I love it here."

The woman returned with their wine, "Enjoy, have you made up your mind or do you need more time?"

Fergus handed her the menus, "We would like the large double meat supremo."

The woman smiled, "That is pop's favorite to make and eat" she said with a laugh.

Lily sipped her wine, "This was a wonderful idea. I love that we don't have to listen to women fighting, or Beverly giving us the stare down while we try to enjoy our meal."

"I'll take care of Beverly. I didn't move over here to be in the middle of women fighting over me." He said with a laugh, "I would have never thought I would be so popular."

"Fergie, you are too funny, you don't realize how funny you are. Tell me about the woman who passed away in your apartment."

"I've heard she committed suicide. According to Lacey and Cookie she would have never done that. Then I hear she was found on the floor of the bedroom with a dildo shoved in her mouth."

Lily set her wine glass down and covered her mouth in shock at the thought, "And that bumbling sheriff called that a suicide?"

"That is what I heard! How crazy is that?"

Mamma is walking toward their table with their pizza. Fergie moved the candle to the side by the window.

"You two enjoy!"

"Thank you, it not only looks amazing it smells wonderful!"

Lily and Fergus couldn't wait to dig in. The front door opened while they placed pizza on their plates. Sheriff Sam walked in with Beverly. She had her arm in his. They didn't notice Lily and Fergus. Lily tapped Fergus' foot with hers, she nodded toward Sam and Beverly as they sat in a booth. Beverly was all smiles and the sheriff looked like he was enjoying her company.

Fergus looked at Lily, “It looks like I’ve been replaced,” he said with a big grin. He then took a big bite of his pizza.

“That woman gets around!” Lily kept watching them, it was like a train wreck, she couldn’t turn away. “Fergie, it looks like they have known each other for a while, doesn’t it?”

“It sure does.”

“I think I have her figured out wrong.”

“Yeah, me too.”

They nearly polished off the whole pizza. More people entered; the tables were filled up. Mamma returned to their table with a takeout container. She laid the bill by Fergus; he laid cash on the table. The two left without being seen by the sheriff or Beverly.

Lily and Fergus arrived back at his apartment, “Fergie, I wonder what that woman is up to. They looked more like they were dating than just friends.”

“She has a way of making things look like they are one way, when they really aren’t.”

Chapter 11:
Fishing

Morning came earlier than Lily was expecting when there was a knock on her door.

"Fergie, you're early." She answered the door with one shoe in her hand, she walked toward the bed putting it on.

"No Lily, you're late. If we don't get a move on, we might not catch any fish today."

Lily grabbed her sweater, hat and sunglasses. "I haven't had my coffee yet."

"I've got you covered." They entered his apartment; the aroma of fresh coffee filled the small kitchen. Fergus had filled up two travel mugs, he grabbed his tackle box handing it to Lily. He carried the two fishing poles and a bucket. They started their walk down to the pier.

There were several people fishing. Fergus saw the same man he had talked to a few days earlier, "Hey buddy, are they biting?"

"Yes, I've caught a couple so far." Fergus looked in his bucket, "Nice!"

Lily and Fergus fished for the next couple of hours. Lily caught her first fish. She was so excited, "Fergie, help!" Fergus helped

Lily reel in a Sheepshead. "Oh my God Fergie, he looks like my uncle Fred!"

"Is your uncle Fred this ugly?"

"No! It's the teeth! I've never seen a fish with human looking teeth. Are we going to eat that?" she wrinkled up her nose as she handed it to him.

"Yes, we are. This guy is going to be tasty!"

"This is so much fun! I didn't know if I would like it or not."

Fergus laughed at her, "I was hoping you would."

They brought the four fish they caught back to the apartment. Fergus cleaned them, seasoned and laid them in a foil lined baking dish. Lily stood by and watched. The two enjoyed their catch for the day.

Later that afternoon

Fergus had called Lacey and Roxie. They were going to meet up at Roxie's apartment #123 across from Fergus' on the other side of the pool. Fergus had a few questions they might know the answers to. Roxie opened her door with a smile, "Come in and make yourselves comfortable. Can I get you something to drink?"

Lily smiles, "Not for me, I'm good."

Fergus sat in an easy chair by the couch, "I'm good as well. We just have a few questions; we won't keep you long."

Lacey was curious, "What can we do for you?"

Lily leaned forward, "What can you tell us about Beverly that we don't already know?"

Roxie chuckled, "She is a very shallow person. She likes to be in charge, apparently, she ran a couple of upscale clothing stores in what we like to call your previous life."

Fergus had a puzzled look on his face, "What do you mean by previous life?"

"Let me answer that one for you." Lacey said with a smile, "In your previous life before retirement you were a homicide detective."

"Oh, ok." Fergus rubbed his chin. "Did she own those stores?"

"I think so, especially with the way she dresses. That woman has some expensive clothing, name brands you only find in high end stores in big cities."

Lily looked at Lacey, "Lacey, do you know if she was married? What happened to her husband? Does she have any family around here?"

"I think her husband died in a car accident at least that's what I've heard. I believe she has an adopted son. I've seen a couple of pictures of a boy and a young man in her apartment. I overheard her saying once that it was her son she adopted when he was a toddler. Her husband was rich; he had family money, which is now Beverly's money."

Fergus looked at both women, "What can you tell us about the local sheriff?"

Roxie crossed her arms, "Not much, I have seen him around town. He has only been here if there is a disturbance or a death. There is a deputy, he works the night shift, so we don't see him much at all." Roxie thought for a moment, "Wait I take that back. I have seen him here out of uniform, I had to look twice before I figured out it was him."

"What was he doing?" Lily asked with interest.

"He was going into the elevator. He had his head down, I'm sure he didn't see me."

Lacey cleared her throat, “I talked to him once, I just said hello sheriff. He didn’t say much, he just nodded. It’s like he would rather be somewhere else than here in Summers Bay.”

Fergus stood up, “Well, I think we have heard all there is. If you think of anything else, you know where I live.”

“Yes, we know.” Lacey replied.

Lily stood, “Fergus I think everyone knows where you live by now. Come on, let's let these ladies get on with their day.”

Roxie opened the door, “I hope we were able to help you.”

Fergus waved as they walked back to his apartment.

Roxie closed her door, “I wonder why they wanted to know about Beverly and the sheriff?”

Lacey shrugged her shoulders, “Who knows? I’m sure they have their reasons.”

Roxie walked over to the couch and sat down, “I wonder if they think Beverly killed Sondra?”

“I think she did, especially after hearing what happened in the dining room. I heard Beverly threatened to kill Sondra in front of everyone there. I have seen Beverly mad before, I think she has it in her to do that. I’m staying far away from her.”

Lacey stood up, “Do you want to take a walk over to the Bistro? We can people watch and maybe see Doug again.”

“Sure, let’s go.”

They walked up to the counter, ordered their wine and carried their glasses to a high-top table close to the isle of traffic. The women hadn’t been there ten minutes before they noticed Doug walking toward them.

“Hello, ladies. Nice to see you again.”

They both smiled, "Have you gotten settled in yet?" asked Lacey.

"Yes, I have thanks. I was just coming down here to grab a sandwich."

"We stopped for a glass of wine before dinner. Why don't you join us?" Roxie said with a smile.

Lacey looked at Doug, "No need to eat alone. Let's have a glass of wine, then we can all go to dinner together. You can tell us all about yourself and what brought you to our community here at 'Sunshine Village'.

Doug agreed, the three of them enjoyed wine and conversation before heading over to the dining room.

Chapter 12: **Windchimes**

Back inside Fergus' apartment, Lily picked up the scent of perfume. Fergus closed his sliding door.

"Fergie, can you smell that?"

"I'm not sure what you're talking about."

"Perfume, it reminds me of my mother's favorite 'White Shoulders'."

"I did notice the smell of perfume right after I moved in, I thought someone was in here. I looked around and the smell went away."

Lily walked into the kitchen, "I wonder if you have a ghostly visitor?"

"Lily, I was kidding when I told you my apartment might be haunted." He said with a laugh.

"I'm serious Fergie, maybe the previous owner is wanting to tell you something."

Fergus laughed out loud, "Lily, do you believe in that kind of stuff?"

"Actually, I do. As you know my mother died tragically when I was small. My dad told me later when I was able to understand what happened. He also told me he would hear me talking to someone when I was put to bed. He came in to check on me one night. He asked who I was talking to. He later told me I said I was talking to mommy. He also told me he smelled her perfume in my room on several occasions."

Fergus scratched his head, "Wow! Do you remember any of that?"

"Sadly no, I think it's because I was told no one was there, that it was my imagination. Children are more open than adults. I wish I could remember."

Lily walked back to the counter stool and sat down, "Would you be open to having someone come in here that could communicate with spirits? Maybe there is something to it. What if you have a ghostly visitor? What if it's Blanche? "Lily rubbed her hands together with excitement.

Fergus rubbed his chin, "I'm not sure. I've never believed in any of that stuff."

"A sensitive, a psychic, a ghost hunter, a medium. I'm sure there is someone around here that does that. Those TV shows are the in thing now on ghost hunting. Let's say there is something to it. Maybe it could help with our little investigation. Would you be open to that?"

"I'm listening."

"What if I do some checking and I find someone that does communicate with spirits. Would you be okay if I made an appointment for them to come over? Come on Fergie, what will it hurt? What if it helps? If we get nothing, at least we tried something. I'm sure you've heard of psychics who have helped solve crimes."

"Yes, I've heard of that before. I've also heard of crackpots out there that charge a small fortune and they turn out to be wrong."

"I agree it's a shot in the dark. Let's give it one shot."

"Okay just one shot and then it's back to what we know, good old detective work."

"Deal!" Lily held out her hand, Fergus shook it.

Fergus stood up, "Come on, let's go talk to Cookie. She knew the lady that had this apartment before me. Maybe she can give us some information."

Cookie's apartment

Cookie opened her door holding Lucy, "Fergus come in, what a nice surprise."

Fergus and Lily walked in; he introduced Lily. Little Lucy made her way to Fergus' lap. Lily told Cookie about the smell of perfume, and it smelled like 'White Shoulders'.

Cookie put her hand up to her mouth with a look of surprise on her face, "That is what Blanche wore all the time, it was her favorite perfume. She visited her old apartment. I've heard it said when someone dies tragically, they may have unfinished business and they revisit the site of their death."

"Where did you hear that if I may ask?" Lily asked with interest.

Blanche and I have an acquaintance, Madame Yvette. She is a medium; we would have her read our cards from time to time. She is the real deal."

"Is she local?"

"She is in Ocean City, it's the next beach town north of us. It's not too far, just fifteen miles."

"Do you have her phone number?"

"Yes, let me get it for you." Cookie walked over to her phone book, "Here it is." She handed a card to Lily, "You can keep the card I have an extra."

"Thanks." Lily tucked the card in her pocket, "You've been a big help."

Fergus stood up handing Lucy back to Cookie.

"I'm not trying to be nosy; I have to ask. Are you going to have her come over and try to reach Blanche?"

Fergus smiled at Cookie, he patted her on her shoulder, "If we do, I'll let you know."

Cookie walked them to the door, "Please, can I be present if you have her come over?" She pleaded, "Blanche was my best friend."

Lily saw the concerned look on her face, "Keep this to yourself, and we'll see."

Cookie nodded her head in agreement.

The detectives headed toward the gym to see who was in the weight room. It was quiet. There were two little ladies with white hair working out with 5lb weights. Lily poked Fergus on the arm, "I don't think these two are our perpetrators." They both chuckled as they walked back to his apartment.

Hazel and Edna noticed they were being watched as they worked out. The sisters went to the gym three times a week; they had done this for years along with walking.

Lily took the card out of her pocket; she made a call to Madame Yvette. She explained to her what had happened in the apartment.

"I would be very happy to help you. You've caught me at a good time. I can be there within the hour if that works for you?" she said in a thick accent.

"Yes, that works for us. We will see you soon."

Fergus made a call to Cookie, "You can come over, the Madame will be here shortly. If you wouldn't mind, leave Lucy home this time."

"Of course, I'll be right over. Thank you."

Cookie gave Lucy a treat and told her, "I'm just going down the hall. You be a good girl and I will be back soon." She gave Lucy a pat on the head before she left.

Madame Yvette arrived with her tools of the trade. She first saged the small apartment, then lit a few candles on the counter. Fergus, Lily, and Cookie watched as she worked.

"Please have a seat, I'm going to try and make contact with Blanche. I need quiet to concentrate." Madame Yvette stood by the counter. She closed her eyes and began to talk out loud, "Blanche, if you can hear me, please give a sign so we know you are present." This went on for several minutes. Fergus was getting antsy. Lily was excited in hopes contact would be made. Cookie had her eyes closed knowing her friend would come through. The sound of windchimes rang inside the small apartment. Madame Yvette called out, "Blanche if that is you, please make that sound again so we know you are here with us."

Fergus was surprised at what he had just heard, Lily poked his arm, "See, I told you she was here."

Madame Yvette shushed them, "I need quiet and concentration." Cookie looked around the small apartment and noticed the patio curtains were moving as if there was a breeze moving them. The patio door was closed. Then the sound of windchimes filled the apartment again. Madame Yvette looked like she was in a trance, her head tilted backward, "Blanche, did someone hurt you?" There was no noise. "Blanche, did someone come into your apartment the night you left this earth? "The sound of windchimes filled the room once again.

"Blanche, do you know who that someone is?" There was silence. "Did a man come into your apartment? "The windchimes got louder. "Blanche, tell me who was here". The room was quiet, the curtains stopped moving. "Blanche, can you give me a clue as to who was here?" There was silence. Madame Yvette looked exhausted, "She's gone, this is common. Once spirit has passed, they aren't concerned with earthly happenings. They have work to do on the other side. In most cases they can lead you to their body. After that this is usually the outcome. We did find out it was a man who came into her apartment."

Lily was excited that contact had been made. Cookie had tears in her eyes. Fergus was still trying to take everything in.

"Madame Yvette, what do we owe you for this? "Fergus asked.

"Blanche was my client and my friend. You owe nothing. I am happy to do what I can to help." She said with her thick accent. She collected her belongings and before she left, she handed Fergus some sage, "You are safe to live here. I'm giving you this to cleanse your apartment. Take care and if you need me again here is my card." Fergus accepted the gift and card.

Cookie wiped the tears from her face. Fergus looked at her with concern, "Are you ok?"

"Yes, I'll be fine. Thank you for inviting me over for this. I miss my friend; it was nice to know she is ok." Fergus handed Cookie his handkerchief. She blotted tears from her face.

Lily said with excitement, “See Fergie, I told you this might work, and it did.”

Fergus opened a bottle of wine, “Cookie, can I interest you in a glass of merlot?”

“Yes, that would be nice. Thank you.”

Lily opened a cupboard, “Fergie, where do you keep your wine glasses?”

“In the next cupboard.”

“These aren’t wine glasses; they are just regular glasses.” She said with a laugh.

“Those are wine, beer, anything you want to put in those glasses.”

Cookie let out a laugh, “I know what to bring over next time.”

Fergus poured the wine, Lily looked around in the cupboard and fridge. She cut up some cheese and sliced a loaf of French bread that she cut into small squares.

“Let’s go out onto the patio.” Lily carried the cheese plate out to the small table. It was beautiful outside. There was a nice breeze. Lily could hear windchimes in the courtyard. She walked out into the courtyard checking out other patio areas and noticed windchimes that hung on nearly every patio, “Fergie, this windchime club, what's up with that? By the looks of it everyone is in that club.” She asked as she walked back to his patio area.

Fergus rubbed his chin, he looked in Cookie's direction, “You know more about this club than I do.” Cookie set her wine glass down, “Blanche was a new member of that club. It’s a sex club. The club provides the members with purple windchimes. You hang them out and leave a door unlocked. A member will come in for whatever you have in mind. Blanche also told me there were married couples in the club which surprised me. Her reply was, it's not cheating if it's a threesome", then she laughed.

Lily sipped her wine, "Really? That sounds a bit risky."

"That is what I told Blanche, she didn't listen to me and look where it got her."

"Who is in charge of this so-called club?"

"It's very secretive, you are a member by invite only. I only know about this because Blanche shared it with me. She told me to keep that to myself. If it was found out that she shared this information with anybody she would be thrown out of the club."

"Or worse," Lily said with concern, "Interesting, very interesting. I wonder if Beverly is a member?"

Cookie smirked, "I wouldn't be surprised if she was the leader."

Fergus tried not to choke on his wine as he let out a laugh, "You and me both Cookie."

All three had a good laugh. Lily was still trying to wrap her head around this club, "If we can identify the apartments with the purple chimes, we will know who a few of the members are. That would be a start to help us identify who is up to no good."

Cookie smiled, "I can pretty much tell you who is in that club. This has been going on for a while. Most of the single ladies are in it, with the shortage of men apparently this was a solution. I have heard this club is a 'hot bed' for STD's no pun intended."

The three of them chuckled. Fergus smiled as he looked at Cookie, "Have you been invited to join?"

"No, and I would never consider such a thing. I tried talking Blanch out of it. I'm not with those 'Diamond Divas' as they call themselves. I have never cared for that group, and I'm sure the feeling is mutual".

Fergus was enjoying the company and noticed Cookie for the first time. She was a very pretty lady and very different from the women he usually attracts.

Cookie stood up, "I really need to get back to Lucy, it's her feeding time. That girl really scolds me if I'm gone too long. Thanks for the wine."

Fergus and Lily stood up, Lily picked up the glasses and took them to the kitchen, "It was nice chatting with you Cookie. I hope to see you again before I head back to Springfield."

Fergus walked with Cookie to the front door, "Lil, I'm going to walk Cookie to her apartment. I'll be right back."

As they walked toward Cookie's apartment. Cookie noticed Beverly rushing down the hallway, "I wonder what she is up to now?" Fergus shrugged, "Who knows, and I really don't care."

Standing at the door of Cookie's apartment, Cookie turns to Fergus," Thank you so much for inviting me over, that meant a lot."

Fergus smiled, "You are most welcome, let's do it again soon without the Madame."

Cookie laughed, "Yes, that would be nice. "She handed Fergus his handkerchief back.

Fergus gave Cookie a hug and a kiss on her forehead, "Tell Lucy hi for me."

Cookie waved as she opened her door.

Lily had finished washing the glasses and put them back in the cupboard. Fergus came in with a smile on his face.

"Fergie, what is up with you?"

"What do you mean?"

"You never smile on purpose."

They both laughed, "You're right I don't. That's from years on the job."

"I get it, so I sense some attraction between you and Miss Cookie." She teased.

"Do you?" Fergus said with a half-smile.

"Yes, I do. I like her, Fergie; I think she would make a nice lady friend for you."

Fergus laughed, "Oh, you do?"

"Face it Fergie you're retired, she's a nice lady. She is someone you could have meals with and go to some of the entertainment shows this place has to offer. You could take her to that cute pizza place we went to. And the best part is her dog loves you."

"Lily, are you matchmaking?"

"Sure, if that is what you want to call it. I'm just telling you what is in front of your face because if I don't point it out, you might miss it."

"I won't miss it; I am way ahead of you. Let's go have dinner. I'm starting to get hungry."

"Me too, I'm going to go back and freshen up, do you want to meet me in the dining room?"

"Sure, I'll grab us a booth."

Lily walked the halls back to her room; she noticed her door was ajar, she nudged it open. Her suitcase had been dumped onto the floor. She walked slowly toward the bathroom. No one was there. Her makeup bag had been emptied into the sink. She slowly opened the closet bifold door. The safe was locked. She opened it up with a sigh of relief her gun was still there. Lily took pictures with her phone. She brushed her hair, picked her lip-gloss out of the sink and applied it to her lips. She then picked up her clothes and put them back into her suitcase. Lily walked to the door, checked the lock, then closed her door and started down the hallway to the dining room.

Chapter 13:
Suspects All Around

Lily noticed Fergus sitting in a booth toward the back. The dining room was starting to fill up. She worked her way through the tables of folks checking out the chef's special on their menus. She slid into the booth.

Fergus saw the look on her face, "What's wrong?"

"Oh, nothing. Just the usual, my room was tossed! I need a glass of wine."

Fergus motioned for the waitperson. He came over with menus. "Two glasses of merlot."

"Of course, sir, I'll have that out to you shortly."

"Really? No one can get into those rooms without a key."

"Maybe Beverly slept with the custodian," Lily said with disgust in her voice.

"Oh, come on, Lil, you don't think she would do this, do you?"

"Fergie, I swear she blinds you. She is more capable of something like this than you know." Lily was obviously shaken.

"Look! That witch is sitting over there in a perfect position to watch us."

Fergus rubbed his chin, "Lil, I'm not blinded by her. I see her for what she is. I think we are getting closer to finding out who killed Sondra, and they might be connected to Blanche's death."

"My money is on Beverly; if she didn't do it, she sure in hell knows who did. She may have even orchestrated it. You know she likes to run things around here."

"Yes, I know, and I also know we have a room full of suspects right now. I understand that woman is under your skin. You need to keep your head straight so you can see beyond her; that's all I'm saying. Look around this room and take notice of who is here and who they are with. We might have clues right in front of us."

The waitperson returned with their wine, "Sir, are you ready to order?"

Fergus nodded, "No, we want to enjoy our wine first; give us a few minutes."

"Of course, sir."

Lily sipped her wine as her eyes darted around the room. She noticed Eugene seated in his usual place, doing what he always does, watching. She also noticed Gary Hart from Springfield seated with a couple of women who hang around Beverly. He seemed to be in deep conversation. Roxie and Lacey were seated in a booth on the other side of the room with a man who Lily hadn't seen before, "Fergie, do you know who is sitting with Roxie and Lacey?"

"I'm not sure; he must be a visitor or someone new."

"These women don't waste much time, do they?" Lily sipped her wine as she gazed around the room.

Brian walked up to their booth, "Mind if I join you two?"

Lily scooted over to make room, "Hi Brian, we can use an extra pair of eyes."

"What are we looking for?" Brian asked with curiosity.

"Anything that looks odd or out of place." Fergus replied.

Brian motioned for the waitperson to bring him a glass of wine. He looked around the room. He noticed Beverly. She made eye contact with him, then held her wine glass up, she smiled as she mouthed "cheers."

"That woman knows we are watching her. It's like she is taunting us."

"You have hit the nail on the head with that one, Brian." Lily looked toward Beverly. She hadn't looked away, still staring at the three of them.

"She is like a dog with a bone. Fergie, are you going to deal with her?"

"In due time. I want to watch her for now."

The wait person returned with a menu and Brian's wine.

Chatter filled the large dining room. Orders were taken. Brian was caught up on the day's events. Lily turned to Brian, "Did you know Blanche or Sondra?"

"I know who they are; I don't personally know them. I try to avoid the drama in this place. I've met a nice lady in Ocean City who I spend time with now and then."

Fergus looked surprised, "This is the first I've heard about this. How long has this been going on?"

"Not long. I met her when I was getting a haircut."

"How did that happen?" Lily asked as she sipped her wine.

"She's my barber. She's cut my hair ever since I moved here. We have gotten to know each other and decided to have lunch one day. We've been seeing each other ever since."

Fergus smiled, "Now I see why the restraining order that you threatened Beverly and her posse with worked."

"I wasn't interested in the women in this place. You saw how they rushed you when you moved in. The way they look at you, all smiles and wide-eyed. Only Labradors and lunatics smile all the time like that."

Lily couldn't control her laughter; it was contagious; all three were laughing out loud.

Brian wiped his mouth with his napkin, "Tell me that isn't true."

"Brian, you got that right. I'll never look at them the same way again. I'll be seeing exactly what you described."

Beverly glared at the three of them, thinking, *what do they think is so funny! To laugh at me in front of my face.* She threw her napkin on her plate, stood up, and walked toward Fergus' booth.

Brian, Lily, and Fergus watched as she got closer. She had fire in her eyes. She slapped her hand on their table, "What is it with you people?"

Fergus started to laugh, "We have no idea what you're talking about."

Lily smiled at her, "Beverly, be careful before you make a fool of yourself again."

Beverly turned her crazed look toward Lily, "Me be careful? Ha! You don't belong here! Fergus, did you find this little tart in town? How much is he paying you for the weekend, dear?"

Lily was mad now; Fergus reached for her hand to stop her from saying anything. He then turned toward Beverly, "I'm going to say this one time only. We are not a thing, and we will never be a thing. You need to walk away now while you still have some dignity left. I don't need to explain my friendships to you or anyone else."

Beverly turned on her heel and walked toward the door. Lily saw Eugene take notice of what had just happened.

Lily's face was red. Brian called the waitperson over for more wine, "Three please."

Fergus looked at Lily, "See I've set her straight now."

"Did you hear what she said? You don't belong here; that is the same thing that was in the note under my door."

"I agree with you, Lil; maybe she did write that note. We don't know if it was her that tossed your room."

The waitperson returned with the wine. People in the dining room were starting to filter out. The noise level had lowered.

Brian shook his head, "That woman needs to take an anger management class."

The three of them laughed in agreement.

Lily watched Eugene as he left his table; he gave her a nod. She smiled back.

"Fergie, you know I have to head back to Springfield in the morning."

"Yes, I figured as much. Your time here went too fast. Come back on your next days off. Let me know when and I can book a room for you."

Lily smiled, "I will be back; you can count on that. You can always call me and keep me up on things."

"You know I will."

The evening ended with a light conversation. Fergus hugged Lily. She headed back to her room to pack; morning would be here before she knew it.

The following morning

Fergus awoke to windchimes that sounded like they were in his bedroom. It was still dark out. The sun was rising on the horizon. The minute his feet touched the floor, the sound quit. He headed toward the kitchen to make a cup of coffee. He carried his mug to the living room, where he sat to watch the early morning news. Before he got settled, there was a pounding on his door. *Now what? Can't a person get some peace and quiet around this place?*

Fergus opened the door to Brian, "What is all the commotion about? Wait, don't tell me you want a cup of my famous coffee."

Brian walked toward the patio blinds and opened them, "Look! I just saw this from my patio."

Fergus walked over to the slider door and noticed there was something white floating in the pool. He sat his coffee on the end table and opened the slider door. He walked out toward the pool, followed by Brian. Fergus called Lily, "Lil, are you still here?"

"Yes, I was just getting ready to walk out to my car. What's up?"

"Come over as soon as you can get here." He hung up the phone.

Lily set her suitcase down and walked down the hall to his apartment. The door was unlocked; she walked in and saw Fergus and Brian out by the pool. She walked toward the men, "Oh my God!" She put her hands over her mouth, "Is that Beverly?"

"I'm not sure; it sure looks like it could be."

Fergus, Brian, and Lily stood as they looked around the pool area. Then their eyes darted around the surrounding apartments to see who, if anyone, was watching, hopefully, to see if there was a potential witness. It was noticed a couple of curtains were opened. There was a man standing on his balcony watching. Fergus's mind was taking in all that was around.

Lily took out her phone, she took pictures of the body and the surrounding area by the pool, "I'll call the sheriff; I'll also call the M.E." The M.E. was first on the scene, followed by paramedics. The body was pulled from the pool. The paramedics worked on her for some time, then called it. It was Beverly in a white nightgown; it appeared to be the same one she wore the night she called Fergus to her apartment. The Sheriff arrived late as usual.

"What do we have here? Looks like she went for a dip." He walked around the body, noticed a broken wine glass by a lounge chair, "I'd say we have a simple case of drowning. Looks like she had a bit too much to drink." He pointed to the empty wine bottle under the table.

The M.E. looked at the Sheriff in disbelief, "She's wearing a nightgown. Doesn't this look suspicious to you, Sheriff?"

"No, it doesn't; I've heard about the parties that go on here with your windchimes and all. Case closed! This looks to be a slip and fall. She couldn't get out of the pool due to her wearing a night dress. Therefore, it's a drowning pure and simple. Don't you have times when the pool is open and closed around here? What about pool rules, bringing glass into the pool area? I can't help it if you people don't read signs." The Sheriff walks toward the gate, shaking his head.

Fergus called out to him, "You know who this is, don't you? You were seen having pizza with her the other day."

The Sheriff turned around, "Are you getting smart with me?"

"Sheriff Sam, if you're not going to do your job, I'm going to call someone in who will."

"Good luck with that one." He turned away and exited through the gate. Sheriff Sam walked to his cruiser parked in front. He got into his car and drove to the side of the building. His hands were shaking; tears filled his eyes. He had known Beverly personally. They were friends, close friends. Friends with benefits, some might call it, "Beverly, what happened to you?" He couldn't hold back the tears that fell; he wiped his face then drove back to the station.

The M.E. and his assistant Kelly placed Beverly in a black bag, zipped it up, and put it on a gurney. He looked at Fergus with concern, "They are dropping like flies around this place. I still have the last one on ice."

Fergus, Lily, and Brian walked back to his apartment. Lily was still shocked by what she just saw, "Fergie, we have to start over now. Unless Beverly threw herself into the pool to throw us off."

Fergus chuckled, "That would be a first, Lil."

"Fergie, I thought you were going to sleep in this morning."

"That was my plan. I woke up to the sound of windchimes in my bedroom."

Lily slaps his arm, "Shut up!"

"Really, Lil, the same we heard when Cookie was here with Madame, What's her name?"

"Too bad you didn't hear them before Beverly wound up in the pool."

Lily pointed to the coffee pot, "Can I get one of those to go? I hate to run. I need to get back to Springfield if I still want my job. I'm just a phone call away."

"Sure, let me get you a travel mug; hey Lil, I'll do some digging around here and see if anyone saw Beverly last night."

She hugged Fergus, "Thanks for the coffee; let me know what you come up with." She shook Brian's hand, "I'll be back as soon as possible."

Lily had time to go over everything in her head as she drove back to Springfield. *First, Sondra, with a stiletto smashed into her eye, then Beverly, face down in the pool. Where does Blanche fit into all this? Motives for murder are usually revenge, money, and sex. Sondra had money; Blanche was waiting for someone to have a sexual encounter with. Beverly was not a nice person. She was hated by a handful. There is a different motive for all three. Could it be one person or three different perpetrators?* Lily's mind raced, going over and over all three deaths. *Who would want Blanche dead? I've heard she had the eye of all eligible gentlemen, so jealousy was there. Beverly is a suspect in my book on that one. Sondra and Beverly got into it in the dining room; Beverly again is suspect. So, who put Beverly in the pool? Roxie and Lacey because they think she killed their friend?*

With her mind running wild with question after question, the drive back to Springfield seemed faster.

Fergus grabbed a few baggies. He went back to the pool area to collect the broken wine glass and the empty bottle. He would later take them to the Medical Examiner's office.

Something isn't right about this. I just don't see Beverly coming down here in her nightgown. I know she has been upset. I know she wanted more from me. I wasn't interested in a relationship at this time. Did that throw her over the edge? Fergus' mind was clouded with questions as to what happened to Beverly and why.

Chapter 14:
Sunshine Village Makes the News

In a small town, news travels very fast. A young reporter, Andrea Day, from the local news station in Ocean City, had listened to her police scanner. She heard of another death at Sunshine Village in Summer's Bay. She made the fifteen-mile drive with her cameraman Stuart.

Andrea felt this was a newsworthy story. Her dream was to be a video journalist for a big news station.

Andrea arrived at nine am; she and Stuart walked into the lobby. They were met by the management, who told them there had been an accident, everything was resolved. Andrea knew when someone was giving her the brush-off. They continued down the hall toward the dining room. Roxie and Lacey were on their way to breakfast when they were stopped.

"Excuse me, ladies, can I ask you a few questions?"

Roxie smiled when she saw the cameraman. She smoothed her hair while she smiled, "Why yes, what can we do for you?"

"I'm Andrea Day from WXLA Daily News. We heard there had been a drowning here. Can you tell us what you know about it?"

Lacey stood next to Roxie, "I heard it was an accident; it couldn't have happened to a better person if you ask me."

Roxie elbowed Lacey, "Beverly was her name; we know it wasn't an accident."

"And how do you know that?"

"Because there have been three deaths here this last month. Sondra, our friend, was said to have been in a household accident, but that's not true. Lacey and I were her best friends. We know she was murdered! I don't care what that Sheriff said; we saw her with our own eyes."

"What exactly did you see?"

"She had a stiletto planted in her eye! The Sheriff called that a household accident. You tell me, why would Beverly go swimming in her nightgown? Especially after hours? Ask anyone around here. They will tell you the same thing."

"Well, thank you, ladies; I will do just that."

Roxie stepped toward Andrea, "Are we going to be on the news?"

"Watch the news at five pm today; it's possible."

Andrea was watching for another possible interview when she noticed Fergus Quimby. She recognized him from Springfield. He solved a murder case there just before his retirement. She nudged Stuart, "Get ready."

Fergus saw the camera and knew he was the next target. Andrea walked up to him with her microphone, "Detective Quimby, how are you this morning?"

"Fine, just fine." He continued to walk toward the dining room.

“Sir, please, can I have just a moment of your time?” She gave him a wide smile.

Fergus stopped, “What can I do for you?”

“I just have a couple of questions, if you wouldn’t mind. It has been brought to our attention that there had been a drowning this morning. What can you share with us? This is the second incident in just a couple of days.”

Fergus put his hands in his pants pockets, “I will tell you, things here are being handled by the local authorities. I’m retired; I moved here to relax and enjoy the fishing this area has to offer.”

“Sir, you must have some knowledge of these two incidents.”

“What I think I know is just speculation at this time. I suggest you check with the local Sheriff; he will be able to give you the answers you’re looking for.” Fergus continued into the dining room.

Andrea stood at the restaurant’s entrance, microphone in hand, “This is Andrea Day reporting for WXLA. I’m here at ‘Sunshine Village by the Sea,’ a resort retirement community. There have been three deaths here in the past few weeks. Residents here believe there is more to the story than they have been told by management and the local authorities. Stay tuned for further details on our five O’ clock news.”

Andrea motioned for Stewart to pack it in, “Let’s go out to the pool for a shot, then over to talk to the sheriff.”

Sheriff’s Office

Andrea and her cameraman arrived at the Sheriff’s office, “Stuart, be ready as we go in the door.” They approached the door; the camera was turned on as they entered. Sheriff Sam was seated behind a desk in a side office. The door was open. He had his head in his hands; he looked to be working on something. A gray-haired lady sat at a desk behind the counter. She walked up to the counter, "What can I do for you young folks?"

"We're here to ask the Sheriff a couple of questions. Is he available?"

"Let me see if he is available to talk to you." She walked to the Sheriff's doorway. Andrea couldn't hear what she was saying. She walked back to the counter. Sheriff Sam closed his office door. "He's busy right now; you can try tomorrow."

"I see. Do I need to make an appointment?"

"No, he's usually around unless he's called out. The best time to catch him is early."

"Thanks; here's my card in case he finds himself free." Andrea laid her card on the counter.

Stuart put the camera away. Andrea gets into her car. She shakes her head, "Busy, my ass! He is blowing us off!"

"Why?"

"I'm going to find out." She started her car and headed over to the Medical Examiner's Office.

Medical Examiner's Office

They arrived and had a better welcome than at the Sheriff's office. Kelly and Doc Thompson agreed to answer questions. Andrea, with microphone in hand, nodded to Stuart, "This is Andrea Day. I'm at the Medical Examiner's Office in Summer's Bay, speaking to Dr. Thompson M.E. and his assistant Kelly, Dr. Thompson, what can you tell us about the three deaths at Sunshine Village?"

"I can tell you the first one, Blanche Smith, was found by housekeeping, deceased. I was told by the Sheriff that it was a suicide. Her family gave permission for an autopsy that determined the cause of death was from natural causes. She suffered a heart attack due to a large rush of adrenaline throughout her system."

"Can you explain what would cause that?"

"Adrenaline is released when something surprises you or frightens you. Say you're watching a scary movie, and it makes you jump or cover your eyes. I'm sure you have experienced that."

"Yes, I understand what you're saying. Blanche Smith was scared to death?"

"That is my opinion as to why she died. It caused a heart attack due to her having heart issues before."

"What can you tell us about the second death? I heard the local Sheriff call it a household accident. What is your take on that?"

Dr. Thompson laughed, "I can't say it was a household accident. She had a stiletto heel planted in her face. I believe someone planted it there."

"Murder? Is that correct? And what about today? A body is found floating face down in the pool dressed in a nightgown. Is that also murder?"

"I didn't say murder; I said someone planted the stiletto in the face of the second victim at Sunshine Village. As far as this morning, the family has been contacted, and hopefully an autopsy will give us more information on what happened."

"Miss Kelly, what do you have to say about these deaths?"

"Personally, I should probably bite my tongue on what I think. I had hoped there would be more work put in by our local authorities. People die, and we are the ones to provide answers as to why. When something looks strange or weird, it needs to be investigated further. I believe with all my heart all three of these deaths need further investigation. That is just me speaking."

"I appreciate your candor. Do you think these deaths are related in any way?"

"Like I said, it should be looked into further by the local authorities; I suggest you ask them."

"Thank you, Dr. Thompson and Miss Kelly; this is Andrea Day with your Daily news."

Andrea and Stuart packed up their equipment. Andrea smiled, "Thanks for the impromptu interview; you both were great."

Sunshine Village made the five O'clock news. Andrea was applauded at work for her newsworthy story. She was told to do a follow-up.

Chapter 15:
What is it about Beverly Johnson?

Beverly Johnson was a tall curvy redhead. She always got what she wanted. She had high hopes of performing on Broadway one day. Dancing was her passion. She found her niche with tap dance when she was a teenager. She auditioned all over town. She was always hired as an extra or for the chorus line. She knew she was better than that. Her attitude was better than yours, which didn't earn her any favors in getting hired.

You could say Beverly was an overachiever. She practiced all the time, which caused an overuse injury in her knees that later turned to arthritis. She continued to tap. She worked through the pain her knees caused her up until she moved to Sunshine Village. She kept her tap shoes just in case she had an opportunity to dance again, which happened when a talent show of residents was announced. She practiced in the gym on the hardwood floor, perfecting her routine, and ended up taking the winning trophy. The pain she experienced was back. She had kept her medication in the freezer so it wouldn't go bad, that had been prescribed by her doctor in New York, which eased the pain and swelling.

Fashion has always been a passion. At one time, she owned a couple of high-end women's boutiques in New York. Beverly did quite well for herself financially.

She had been married for several years to her college sweetheart Blake Johnson. When she found out she couldn't have children, they adopted a toddler, two-year-old Oliver. He was the center of her universe.

Blake came from a wealthy family. He was a stockbroker in New York. He was working late one evening when he was hit head-on by a wrong-way driver on his way home. He didn't survive. Oliver was six years old at the time he lost his father.

After losing her husband, Beverly became overprotective of her son. Oliver began to rebel in school, not being able to do things with friends because his mother felt it was unsafe or too dangerous. She would tell him, "Oliver, I'm just doing my job as a mother keeping you safe."

Oliver went to college out of state to be on his own. Beverly devoted her life to him. He was ungrateful in her mind. Oliver felt smothered and just wanted to experience life without his mother breathing down his neck. After college, he moved to Illinois, where he accepted a job in banking. He married a local girl, and they had a son. Oliver kept in touch with his mom on special days and made it a point to call her periodically.

Beverly wanted a relationship with her son like her friends had with their children. She couldn't understand why Oliver had pushed her away. She dove into her work until she was able to retire. She found Sunshine Village to be a place where she could thrive; she had high hopes of finding love and possibly getting married again.

Sunshine Village was a fresh start. She bought her condo with cash and made several improvements starting with color on the walls, removing the carpet, and having hardwood put in. She special ordered draperies to frame her windows. It had to be perfect! Beverly knew exactly what she wanted, and she was going to get it.

Being a businesswoman, she knew how to run things. She immediately got involved with starting clubs for singles. Being president of these clubs made her feel important again, and she made sure others knew just how important she was.

The single woman in the village looked up to Beverly for the way she carried herself. That woman knew how to dress; she didn't go unnoticed, that's for sure. The clubs were filling up with new members. Once again, Beverly was in charge; it was a win for her.

Sheriff Sam had visited the village now and again, checking in with management when he noticed Beverly. She had walked by him on her way to the library. Sam was in awe; she was gorgeous. The smell of her perfume was captivating. He was going to make an introduction before he left.

Beverly was looking for a good book to check out; she enjoyed a good mystery. She liked to read before she retired in the evening. She went to reach for a book when Sam intervened, "Let me help you with that, ma'am." Beverly turned and saw Sam holding her book. She smiled, "Why aren't you helpful? And easy on the eyes too." Sam blushed, and he returned the smile.

She was always taken by a man in uniform. Sam held the book out for her as he introduced himself. Beverly was still smiling, enjoying the attention. She gave him a flirty smile and thanked him.

"How about you let me take you to lunch? I know a great little place. We can get to know one another." She agreed. That was the beginning of their friendship. Sam and Beverly saw each other as often as they could. He was a few years younger than her, but she didn't mind the age difference. Beverly wanted to keep their relationship quiet just between them. She didn't want it to get in the way of looking for her future husband. Beverly called him her boy toy. Sam had hoped for more and thought she might change her mind as time went on. He found out she was pursuing a retired detective who had recently moved in. Sam wasn't going to give up on her. There was something about her that drove him crazy. He didn't know what it was; he couldn't keep away from her. She was like a drug to him; he needed her.

Beverly enjoyed keeping their relationship quiet. It made it more exciting. Sam, on the other hand, didn't like sneaking around. "Bev, when can we stop this charade? I want to show you off as my girl."

Beverly kissed his cheek, "You are such a romantic; that is what I love about you."

"I'm serious; I don't want to sneak around anymore. We're both single; let's act like it. I'm crazy about you."

"Sammy, you know how I feel about you. Isn't that enough? Why do you want to ruin things?"

"I just want to be out in the open with our relationship; I feel like I'm having an affair with a married woman."

Beverly hugged Sam, "Oh, come on now, don't feel that way. What we have is fun and exciting. Just enjoy what we have."

Sam held her close and kissed her. Just holding her wasn't enough, "Bev, I want to marry you."

"I know, maybe one day, Sammy, maybe one day."

Sam felt hopeful. That was one of the last conversations they had.

Chapter 16:
Medical Examiner's Office

Fergus arrived early to bring what he had collected from the pool area. Doc Thompson marked it and had it ready to go to the lab for analysis. There might be something there, and if there was, it could be discovered through forensics.

"Good morning, Fergus; seeing we have someone on the job is nice."

"No matter how hard I try to retire, it seems there is always something there to stop mc."

"We have Beverly's son coming in later today. He has given permission to autopsy the body. Apparently, he and his mother had been estranged for quite a few years. He had hoped to reconnect with her. Unfortunately, that will never happen."

"Kelly and I will be performing the autopsy this morning. We performed the autopsy on Sondra Miller."

"Were you able to find anything?"

"The hit to the back of her head was not the cause of death. However, it was hard enough to knock her off her feet. The stiletto that penetrated her eye was the death blow. With that being said, I did get the report back from the lab. There weren't any fingerprints or DNA on the heel or the trophy."

"What about the button and the white hairs that were collected?"

"Nothing on the button. It could be from a man's or a woman's shirt. The hair didn't have any roots attached, so DNA could not be found there. This was not a household accident as the Sheriff would like to think. This is now considered a homicide. I have notified the Sheriff's office with my findings."

"I guess time will tell if he plans on checking into it or not. Did you find any family?"

"Sondra didn't have any family listed on her card at the village; she did, however, have her affairs in order. Her body was picked up yesterday."

"What happens to her apartment, I wonder?" Fergus looked concerned.

"From what we know, it goes back to the village and is resold. Her things will be donated to a local thrift shop. Or the village might want to keep her furnishings and sell the it furnished."

Fergus rubbed the back of his neck, "Wow, it makes you want to make sure you have your affairs in order, doesn't it?"

"Yep."

"I will leave you to your work. Let me know if you find anything interesting."

"Will do."

Mid-morning

Oliver Johnson arrived before noon. This was something he wasn't looking forward to. Introductions were made. Oliver sat in the chair in front of Doc Thompson's desk.

"First off, I want to let you know your mother drowned. She had chlorine water in her lungs."

"What happened?" Oliver had a puzzled look on his face; he ran his hand throug his hair. "My mother wasn't a great swimmer, but she knew enough not to drown in a swimming pool. I don't see my mother going for a swim in her nightgown after hours. Is it possible she is a victim of foul play?"

"I've sent samples off to the lab, and that should give us a better understanding of what happened. From what I could tell from the autopsy, there wasn't anything unusual I could find other than the drowning that could cause her death."

"How long will it take to get the lab results?" Oliver asked with a concerned look on his face. "Could this be a homicide? Did someone kill my mother? "Oliver's eyes welled with tears.

"I can't answer that question right now. I will call you with the lab results as soon as I get them in. It shouldn't take too long. Will you be staying in town?"

Oliver stood, "I am going to go to my mother's apartment. I'll be staying there." Oliver handed Doc his card." You can contact me at that number." He shook Doc's hand and left.

Doc opened his file cabinet and placed Beverly's file among the others. As he closed the cabinet, he motioned to Kelly, "Let's get an early lunch. We need a break."

Chapter 17:
Hazel and Edna

Sisters

The sisters heard about Beverly through the gossip grapevine. With Sunset Village filling up, the gossip was plenty.

"Sister, would you please bring the coffee creamer when you sit down." Edna put her pink packet of sweetener into her cup, stirring with her spoon.

"Of course, sister. Are we going to have toast this morning, or are we going to the dining room for breakfast?"

Hazel brought her coffee cup to the table with the coffee creamer, "I think we should go to the dining room. I read there is a new special on the menu."

Edna poured the creamer into her coffee cup and smiled, "The atmosphere around here has been nice lately, don't you think, sister?"

"Why, yes, it has. Isn't it amazing what a little housekeeping can do?" Hazel smiled as she sipped her coffee.

Edna checked the monthly activities in the circular, "It's a shame about Beverly; who will take over the clubs?"

Hazel brushed a stray hair away from her face, "I imagine there would be a vote among the members. Maybe the clubs will die out. The 'Sunset Sisters' was just a place where Beverly told the ladies who and who they couldn't pursue."

"She won't be telling anyone anything from now on, will she?" Edna and Hazel laughed, "Sister, we shouldn't make fun of the departed."

"I can't understand for the life of me why she was looked up to. She was turning this place into a 'hussy town'! She was becoming known as the village pump!" Edna was starting to get upset.

"Calm down, sister; she is gone now. Things will settle down. Don't let yourself get all worked up. Take a breath, and let's just get on with our day."

Edna nodded, "You're right, sister. Let's finish our coffee and go to breakfast."

Dining room

The sisters sat at their usual table; they ordered the new special and chatted as the residents filled the tables and booths. Thcy noticed Eugene seated at his usual table in the back.

"Poor Eugene, he has eaten alone since his Joan passed. What do you think he does all day?" Edna laid her napkin in her lap.

"I don't know; maybe he will meet a nice lady to help him pass the time. Heaven only knows we have plenty of single ladies who live here."

The sisters finished their breakfast, sipping their coffee, when they noticed Roxie and Lacey looking for a table, "Those two don't look worse for wear after they lost their friend Sondra. They seem to be doing fine." Edna made eye contact with Roxie and smiled. Roxie waved at the sisters.

Hazel elbowed Edna, "See, those two are enjoying themselves. I noticed Sondra was a bit pushy when the three of them were together."

Edna dabbed the corners of her mouth with her napkin, "Remember what mother always told us. Two's company, three's a crowd."

"Yes, I remember. Mother always seemed to have a saying. You left the end off of that, fours too many and fives not allowed."

"I left the end off on purpose sister. She always told us to keep our house clean too; a little housekeeping never killed anyone, she would say." The sisters laughed.

"She didn't know the way we clean house." More laughter.

The sisters were like two giddy school girls, laughing at their own jokes.

Courtyard

After breakfast, the sisters took a walk around the grounds. They walked by the pool and noticed it looked as if nothing had happened there. There was a new calm, and the morning breeze felt nice. "This is what we moved here for; isn't it nice?"

Hazel sighed, "This is nice, sister."

The sound of windchimes tinkled with the breeze, Hazel stopped to look around the courtyard, and she noticed a couple of patios had purple windchimes hanging out.

Edna looked at her sister, "What are you looking at?"

"Those sex chimes! Everyone around here knows what they are for. It's not a secret anymore."

"Hopefully, that club will die out now that Beverly is gone." Edna nudged her sister to continue their walk.

"Was she the head of that club too?" Hazel asked with a sour look on her face.

"I'm not sure; I would guess she could have been."

"There needs to be a stop put to that! Half the people walking around here probably have some disease that is just waiting to be diagnosed!" Hazel said in disgust.

The sisters continued their walk toward their apartment, greeting residents along the way. Fergus was walking toward them in the hall, "Good morning, ladies."

Edna and Hazel stopped, "Good morning, where is your girlfriend?"

Fergus smiled, "I think you're talking about Lily; she was my partner in Springfield. She is now the lead homicide detective there. We are just friends."

Hazel poked Edna, "See, I told you she wasn't his girlfriend."

Fergus laughed with them, "You ladies, have a good day."

"Mr. Fergus," Hazel called after him, "You too."

The sisters reached their apartment going inside. Hazel looked at Edna, "Don't you find that interesting that Mr. Fergus had his homicide partner here for a visit?"

"What do you mean?"

"Do you think they are working together on the deaths that have happened here?"

"I never thought about it until you just brought it up. Do you think Sheriff Sam has them working for him?"

Edna looked at her sister, "That could mess up the house cleaning that goes on around here."

Hazel smiled as she walked toward the living room and sat in her favorite chair, “I wouldn’t worry yourself. Things have calmed down for now. Just sit back and enjoy it while you can.”

“You’re right, sister.” Edna walked over to the patio door, looking out toward the pool.

Chapter 18:
Changes

Management had been under pressure since Beverly Johnson was found floating face down in the pool. Residents were feeling unsafe. There was talk about several residents planning to move. Graffiti had been spray painted on the driveway 'move in and die.' Changes had to be made.

Flyers were posted about a 60's pool party hosted by Sunshine Village. A BBQ was planned, along with beer and wine. There will be a live band, prizes for the best costumes, and a dance contest. This should help with morale and get residents to move forward after the unfortunate events that have taken place in the past few weeks. The party was this coming Saturday.

Excitement was in the air; residents were talking about the upcoming party. Management was happy the mood had changed in a more positive way. They decided to host four parties a year. Residents would be able to vote for the types of parties and holidays they were interested in.

Fergus invited Cookie over to his apartment for a fish fry; he had caught four fish that morning and wanted the company to help him eat his catch. Cookie was excited to be invited. She arrived with potato salad, wine, and wine glasses.

Fergus opened his front door to see Cookie with her arms full, "Let me help you with that." He smiled as he took the wine and wine glasses, "I see you brought wine glasses."

"I told you last time I knew what to bring over the next time I was invited." Cookie set the salad on the counter, "Fergus, those are a gift for you."

Fergus was happy that Cookie accepted his invitation and was grateful for her thoughtfulness. "Let me open this wine; we have time to enjoy a glass before I start the fryer up." He poured two glasses of merlot.

Cookie held her glass up as she looked at Fergus, "Here's to our health and a long friendship, cheers." Fergus touched his wine glass to hers, "cheers."

The two talked for about an hour before Fergus decided to fry the fish. It felt as if they had known each other for years. It was nice to be able to talk and enjoy each other's company without expectations.

As the two friends enjoyed their dinner, Fergus brought up the 60's party that was coming up, "How would you like to be my date for the pool party?"

"I would be honored," Cookie said with a wide smile, "I'll have to go through my closet and pull out my hippie clothes."

"So, you were a hippie?"

"Not really; I did like the boho style of the clothes. What about you?"

"No, I was what you probably referred to as a nerd." They both laughed.

"Fergus, I can't see you as a nerd."

"I was studious; science and math were my strong suits. I didn't have a pocket protector or anything." He said with a laugh, "I was more into getting good grades, and I was a member of the camera club."

Cookie sipped her wine as Fergus enlightened her about what he did in the '60s.

"I did have a really nice convertible Volkswagen while others rode on skateboards." He chuckled.

"I'll bet you were popular with the girls."

"Just the neighbor girl who rode to and from school with me."

"No girlfriends?"

"I didn't say that I had a couple of girlfriends. My last high school girlfriend that I had became my first ex-wife."

"Oh, I see. So, you've had more than one wife?"

"Yes, I've had two. After the second one, I thought it was time to throw in the towel."

"I find it hard to believe you gave up so easily."

"It was better for me to throw a few clothes into a laundry basket and walk away. My work as a detective kept me busy working long hours and being on call, which made it difficult to have a social life until now."

"I can see that from what I've seen going on here around us. Your work was solving the mystery of who did what to whom."

"Exactly!"

The fish was cooked to perfection, and Cookie's potato salad was the perfect side. The conversation came easy for the two of them. The more they talked, the more they found they had in common.

Cookie stood up and started putting the dishes into the sink. Fergus helped clear the counter, "Don't worry about the dishes; I'll get them."

"Nonsense! You cooked. I'll clean." She filled the sink with soapy water, "Finish your wine, please."

Fergus did as he was told, and the two continued to chat. Fergus enjoyed Cookie's company. He knew they would see more of each other.

Front Desk

Roxie decided to ask about Sondra's apartment. She was advised it would be up for sale soon.

"I'm very interested in purchasing that apartment with everything in it."

Malissa, the sales representative, was pleasantly surprised to hear that, "Will you be putting yours up for sale or renting it out?"

"I would like to sell mine, furnished. I will remove my personal items."

Malissa looked through a folder, "Let me come up with a price for you on both apartments, and we will see what we can do."

"Wonderful; I'm looking forward to hearing from you soon."

Roxie's apartment

Roxie was all smiles as she turned and walked toward her apartment. She had gone through the numbers and knew this was going to work out. She didn't want Sondra's things to be donated to a thrift store, "Sondra, I will take care of your things. You know I loved your apartment and décor style."

Roxie no sooner walked into her apartment when Lacey knocked at the door, "Roxie, are you home?"

Roxie opened the door and let her in, "I was just going to get ready to go down to the pool. Do you want to join me?"

"You mean the death pool?"

"Roxie, they drained the pool and cleaned it. Really it's ok to go in." she said with a laugh, "Come join me. It's a beautiful sunny day out."

"I guess I'll go get changed and meet you down there. I'll bring us something to drink."

Roxie walked Lacey to the door, "Save me a chair." Lacey waved, "Will do."

She was excited and wanted to tell Lacey her news but knew she had to wait until it was confirmed she would get the apartment. Roxie would just need to pack a couple of boxes and suitcases; it would be an easy move.

At the pool

Lacey pulled two lounge chairs close to each other next to a side table. She laid her towel out on her chair and placed her small cooler under the table. There were only a few people at the pool. The gate opened. Roxie smiled as she walked toward the two chairs, "Isn't this the life? She laid her towel on the lounge.

"I brought tanning lotion; what did you bring for drinks? I'm thirsty."

"Wine coolers" Lacey reached into the cooler pulling one out for her.

"Thanks." She takes a sip, "Nice and refreshing."

Lacey looked at Roxie, "This feels strange to be out here knowing Beverly took her last dip in the pool."

"Lacey, you know if that had been you or I floating face down in that pool, Beverly wouldn't give us a second thought, and if she did, she would say something to the effect of, 'It was a natural death, she went swimming and naturally died.' You have to forget about her."

"Roxie, you know how to make me laugh. She probably would say something like that right before she went into the pool."

"She was a piece of work, wasn't she?"

Lacey opened her wine cooler, "I think she was hated by just about every woman in this place."

"I didn't hate her."

"Oh, come on now." Lacey smirked, "You are one lying bitch" she said with a laugh.

"I may have prayed for her death now and again, but no, I didn't hate her."

Lacey laughed loud enough that people down at the other end of the pool looked in their direction, "You are too funny, girl!"

Roxie looked serious, "I've stopped stressing over shitty people. Beverly was not a nice person. I decided to leave all her clubs, and just enjoy what we have around us."

"Roxie, don't forget I walked out of that meeting with you and Sondra. That woman was not going to tell me what I could and couldn't do. Let's stop talking about her. She's not worth the space she's taking up in my head. Besides, I'm ready to get into the pool."

Lacey stood up and walked to the pool; as she dipped her toes into the water, she turned toward Roxie, "You're right; the bitch is dead."

Roxie walked toward the deep end and dove in.

Fergus' apartment

The dishes had been cleaned up. Cookie walked toward the counter where Fergus sat on a stool with his wine, "I want to thank you for a wonderful lunch; the fish was wonderful!"

"Thanks for bringing the potato salad. It was delicious!"

"I've always enjoyed cooking. As you know, when we live here, we don't do that as much anymore."

"That gives us time to do other things together." Fergus stood up and walked toward Cookie. She was feeling a bit nervous as he got closer. He leaned in and kissed her.

She was surprised, probably because she wasn't expecting it. She looked up at him, "Wow!" They both broke out into laughter. "Would you please do that again?"

Fergus put his arms around her and kissed her again, this time with a little more passion.

"I've gotta admit that is better than doing dishes."

"I agree wholeheartedly."

She looked up at him with a wide smile, "I hate to leave just when we are getting warmed up."

"Then don't; let's have another glass of wine and finish off the bottle."

"Fergus, Lucy isn't going to understand why I was late feeding her."

"Ah yes, Little Lucy. Next time you come over, bring her." He walked her to the door.

"I will; she has really taken to you." Fergus opened the door, and as she turned to walk toward her apartment, she looked back and blew him a kiss. Fergus smiled and waved.

Chapter 19:
Beverly's Apartment

Oliver sat on the couch, looking through old photos. He stopped at one with him and his father. He was helping his dad wash the car. Oliver was holding the hose and spraying his father instead of the car. He smiled as he turned each page, holding treasured memories of his childhood before his father passed. He closed the photo album and placed it into a box. It was bittersweet going through his mothers' things, finding all the mementos she had kept of his years growing up. His eyes filled with tears as he held a picture of her, "I wish we had reconnected before you passed. You had a way about you that I just didn't care for. Some would call it controlling; you called it mothering. You called me rebellious; I was independent, and that didn't sit well with you." He placed his mother's picture in the box atop the photo albums.

Oliver walked into his mother's bedroom. It was very feminine. She was found in the pool in her nightgown, yet her bed was still made. Her apartment looked more like a photo in a magazine; everything was neat and clean. He looked around not knowing where to start, "Mother, what happened to you?" He turned and walked back into the living room when the doorbell rang. He opened the door to two ladies with white hair, "Hi, I hope we're not intruding. We brought you a casserole." Oliver smiled at the ladies, "I'm Oliver, Beverly's son." Edna and Hazel nodded, "Yes, we heard you were here. We wanted to make sure you got something to eat and to let you know how sorry we are for your loss." Oliver accepted the casserole, "And you are?"

"Sister, where are our manners? I'm Edna, and this is my sister Hazel. We were friends of your mothers."

"This was very thoughtful of you; thanks again."

The sisters smiled, "It's the least we could do. If you need anything, we are just down the hall in apartment #210." They both smiled as they turned away.

Oliver closed the door and set the casserole in the fridge. He noticed on the top were taped instructions for heating it up. He was touched by knowing his mother had such nice friends. He looked in the fridge. There wasn't much of anything, just a few bottles of wine. He opened the freezer and noticed a Ziplock bag filled with prescription medication. He looked at each one to see what she had. There were pills for anxiety and sleep; some had the labels removed but were marked with a sharpie on top stating what they were for. He put them back into the freezer, wondering, *why were you keeping all of this in the freezer?* He walked into the bathroom and noticed an empty prescription bottle in the trash. He picked it up and saw it was the medication his mother had taken for years, off and on, for the pain and swelling in her knees from her years of tap dancing. *Her knees must have been bothering her again.*

Oliver heard his phone buzz on the kitchen counter, "This is Oliver Johnson."

"Hi, Oliver; this is Dr. Thompson at the Medical Examiner's Office."

"Hello doctor, do you have any news?"

"Yes, I would prefer it if you would come down to my office so I can share the findings with you."

"Of course, doctor; what would be a good time?"

"I'm available in about an hour. Will that work for you?"

"Yes, I'll see you then."

Medical Examiner's Office

When Oliver arrived at the M.E.'s office, he was met by Doc Thompson, Kelly Anderson's assistant, and a man whom he had not seen before. Doc Thompson shook Oliver's hand, "I'd like you to meet Fergus Quimby." Oliver extended his hand forward. The men shook hands, "Fergus is a retired homicide detective from Springfield and has been helping me with your mothers' case."

Oliver looked puzzled, "Aren't the local authorities working on the case?"

Doc Thompson put his hands in his white doctor's coat, "Unfortunately, no."

"And why not?" Oliver's face flushed red.

"Because our sheriff said it was an accident, a slip and fall."

"And what do you say, doc?"

"That is why Fergus Quimby is helping me look deeper into the evening your mother was out by the pool. I have sent samples that Fergus collected at the scene and samples from the autopsy."

Doc Thompson motioned for Oliver to have a seat. Oliver walked over to the desk area and sat down. Doc Thompson was holding a manila folder; he took a seat at his desk. Kelly and Fergus stood close by. Doc Thompson opened the folder, "I have a couple of questions for you. You may or may not be able to answer them.

"Sure, doc, I will answer what I can."

"Do you know what medications your mother took on a regular basis?"

"I just found her medications in a Ziplock bag in her freezer. I think she was keeping them in case she needed them. I did find an empty prescription bottle in her trash can. It was something that she had taken for years for pain and swelling in her knees."

"Do you know what the name of that prescription is? Can you get me the bottle? I would like to see the bag that is in the freezer as well."

"Yes, I can do that. The one that was thrown away was for what she called Gouty Arthritis. I'm not sure what the name of the prescription is. I know it started with a 'C.'"

Doc Thompson looked inside the folder, "The lab found Colchicine residue in the bottle of wine she had taken to the pool and on pieces of her broken wine glass. Could this be the drug your mother was taking for her knees?"

"Yes, the minute you said the name, I knew that is what she had taken for years."

"Did the doctor that prescribed this medication for her put her on a special diet?"

"Not that I ever remember hearing. She ate pretty much whatever she wanted."

Doc Thompson closed the folder, "What about alcohol? Did your mother drink regularly?"

"She liked her glass of wine; in fact, there are still several unopened bottles in her fridge. I remember her and my dad drinking whisky every now and then."

Oliver looked over at Fergus and Kelly, "Did my mother commit suicide, or did someone kill her?"

Fergus saw the hurt look on Oliver's face, "I don't believe your mother committed suicide. There was no note; besides, she kept herself busy running her clubs and entertaining."

Oliver then looked at Doc Thompson, "Then someone killed my mother. Is that what your report shows?"

"I'm afraid so; she had a large amount of colchicine in her system. This drug, when overdosed, causes nausea, stomach pain, muscle weakness, and fainting, which probably made her fall into the pool. Shallow breathing and a slow heart rate. In older patients' confusion is also a symptom."

Oliver's eyes welled up, "Who would do this to her? And why?"

Fergus cleared his throat, "That is what we are going to try to find out."

Doc Thompson looked at Oliver, "It depends on the amount of Colchicine she ingested; overdose symptoms are delayed up to a week."

Oliver stood up, "I'll get those prescription bottles to you. "Oliver walked over toward the door, "Thank you for your help, Mr. Quimby."

Fergus nodded as Oliver walked out the door.

Doc Thompson stood up, "I wasn't looking forward to that. He seemed to take the news pretty well. I could see the hurt on his face. I don't think Beverly would have taken a huge dose of that medication on her own."

Fergus rubbed his chin, "I guess we have to look at who had been around her this past week. Who would she trust enough to get close to her medications? I'll see what I can find out."

Chapter 20:
A Week Before Beverly Went for a Swim

Edna and Hazel were inside their apartment. Edna set her purse on the counter, "I am so tired of those women fighting. It's time to do some house cleaning!"

Hazel put the tea kettle on, "I agree; this has been going on too long. Did you find anything in her bathroom?"

"As a matter of fact, I did," Edna said in a devilish voice. She pulled a Kleenex out of her pocket to show her sister; it contained a good number of pills. Edna folded the Kleenex back up.

"Oh, goodie!" Hazel said with excitement. "What are they?"

"Pain pills; since she's been a pain, I thought these would be appropriate."

"When shall we start our house cleaning," Hazel asked as she rubbed her hands together like an excited child.

"No time better than the present."

Edna handed Hazel a pair of gloves. "Here, put these on."

Beverly's apartment

Beverly's knees were giving her a fit, so she went into the bathroom to take a pill for the pain. She opened the bottle and saw she only had two pills left.

'That's strange. I could have sworn I had close to a whole bottle.'

"Huh, I must be mistaken. I think I have another bottle in the freezer." She took her pills with a swallow of wine. She changed her outfit, fixed her makeup, and headed down to the restaurant.

House Cleaning

Edna peeked out into the hall and saw Beverly walk toward the elevator. Edna called to Hazel in a loud whisper, "Sister; it's time; let's go."

The sisters scurried out of their apartment toward Beverly's. watching along the way to make sure they weren't seen. Hazel tried the doorknob; it was unlocked. They went inside and closed the door quietly.

Up at the kitchen counter, Edna opened the Kleenex that contained the pills. Hazel looked on over her shoulder, "Hazel, be a dear and get me something to smash these with." Hazel opened a drawer with kitchen utensils and found a small meat tenderizer, "Try this." She handed it to her sister. Edna was able to crush the pills down to dust using the flat side of the utensil.

Hazel opened the fridge taking out a bottle of wine, "Let's use this one; it's one of her favorites." She handed her sister the dark bottle that had been opened. Edna deposited the crushed pills into the wine, then gave the bottle a few swirls to mix them up.

Handing the bottle back to Hazel, she put the cork back in and placed it back into the fridge. Edna wiped the meat tenderizer off with the kitchen cloth and placed it back into the drawer. Hazel checked the hallway, "Coast is clear; let's move."

The sisters quietly slipped back into their apartment and clapped their hands," We did it!" Hazes said with a huge smile. They prepared themselves to go down to the restaurant.

The night of Beverly's pool party

Beverly was feeling down; Fergus had been ignoring her. Her thoughts were running wild. *How could he treat me this way when my mother raised me to be admired? Who is that woman he is spending time with? Why won't he call me? We shared such a wonderful evening together.* Beverly kept going over the night she had dinner with Fergus and how he tenderly made love to her. *I know he wants me; I just know it. It's that woman she is the one keeping him from me.*

Beverly walked over and opened the fridge. She pulled out a bottle of her favorite wine. It was half full. She wanted to finish the bottle off before it went bad. She reached for a wine glass from the cupboard and poured herself a healthy pour. Setting her wine on the countertop, she put on her white silk nightie, the one she wore for Fergus; *he couldn't resist me when he saw me in this.* She smiled at the memory when the phone rang.

"Hello," there was no answer; she could hear that the line was open, and someone was breathing.

"Hello," she said again, still no answer.

"Fergus? Is that you, darling? Talk to me; I want to see you and be in your arms again. I'm lonely; come take up my time." She said in a baby voice, "I miss your touch."

The other end was silent except for breathing. Hanging on, hoping that Fergus is on the other side of her phone call. She spoke in her sultry tone, "Meet me down by the pool, I have something for you." The call ended with a click. Her caller ID showed 'private' as the caller.

She finished her glass of wine and checked the time; it was past midnight. She then slipped on a pair of kitten-heeled slippers. She picked up her wine bottle and glass and headed for the door.

She felt a little dizzy as she walked toward the elevator. Her stomach had been upset earlier. The pain in her knees still bothered her after all these years; she eased her pain with meds and wine. She exited the elevator. The hallway was quiet. She walked toward the exit door, out onto the courtyard. No one was around; the grounds were quiet. All you could hear was the click, click, click of her heels as she entered the gate to the pool area. She picked out a chair so she could watch Fergus's apartment.

There was a light on in the living room. She poured herself another glass of wine and sipped while keeping an eye to see if he would walk out his sliding door. She noticed a shadow of movement then the light was turned off.

She poured the last of the wine into her glass, and she called out, "FERGUS, FERGUS, COME OUT AND PLAY WITH ME."

Her words were slurred. Then she started to laugh, "COME OUT, COME OUT WHEREVER YOU ARE."

She polished off her wine. As she stood up, the glass slipped out of her hand, breaking on the cement by her chair, "OH DARN FERGUS, NOW LOOK WHAT YOU MADE ME DO!"

She was feeling weak; she laughed again. "IF YOU'RE NOT COMING OUT TO PLAY, I'M COMING OVER THERE."

She started to walk toward the gate; her legs were not cooperating; she stumbled, and trying to catch herself, she tipped to the side. The wine bottle fell, rolling under the table. Her legs gave way as she fell into the pool. She splashed at the water, trying to reach the side to pull herself out; her muscles were not cooperating.

This went on for several minutes before she tired out. Trying to keep her head above water was fruitless. Her face fell below the water line; her body gave up. Panic set in. She looked at the bottom of the pool, trying to lift her head, holding her breath until she no longer could. She took a breath; water filled her lungs. She suddenly had a feeling of peace as she floated face down.

Chapter 21:
Lily Returns

The weekend was approaching, and Fergus had yet to figure out what he was supposed to wear to the pool party. He decided to call Lily and fill her in on the recent autopsies. Afterward, he could ask her for advice about the party. He sat up at the counter and opened his flip phone when it rang. He saw it was Lily.

"Hello, Lil; you're not going to believe this. I was going to call you."

"Really?" Lily said with a smile in her voice, how funny. I just got off the phone with Dr. Thompson."

"I was going to bring you up to date on the autopsies. It looks like Doc is one step ahead of me."

"Yes, he told me that Beverly's son had brought in all the medications he found, including the empty bottle that was in the bathroom. He wants to talk to both of us about the findings from the lab."

"Are you planning a trip this way?"

"I am. Please book me a room at your resort for this weekend?"

Fergus smiled, "I would be happy to. It just so happens there is a 60's pool party this weekend. Bring your hippie clothes. There will be a contest."

"That sounds like fun!"

"I have a little problem I could use your help with."

"Sure, what's up?"

"I have no idea what to wear to this darn thing; I was hoping that you might be able to help me out."

Lily giggled, "I would be delighted to help you out. Just give me your sizes."

"I don't want to look silly; I'm trusting you."

"You leave it to me; I will have you looking groovy in no time." She laughed, "Don't worry, I've got you covered."

Fergus knew he could count on his partner, "Thanks, Lil; I'll see you soon. Drive safe."

"Not to worry, I'll text you when I'm getting close."

"No, don't text, call, I can't do all that crazy stuff."

"Okay." She laughed at him, "I'm going to give you a lesson in texting when I see you."

Fergus groaned, "I don't know about that; we'll see."

"Are you going to be grumpy?"

"No, I'm going to be me."

"Goodbye, Fergie." Lily smiled and shook her head, "What will I do with you?"

Lily arrived late afternoon on Friday. Fergus met her in the lobby and made sure she got to her room.

"Once you get settled, come over. We will go to the M.E.'s office. He's expecting us."

It didn't take long for Lily to put her things in her room. She was at Fergus' apartment in no time. Fergus opened the door, "Wow! That was fast!"

"I'll unpack later; I am curious as to what the doc has to say."

"This should be interesting; let's go."

The M. E.'s Office

It was the end of the day for Doc Thompson and Kelly. Doc had a manila folder on his desk.

Fergus and Lil arrived and were greeted by Doc, "Thanks for coming by. It's great to see you both. Have a seat if you would." He picked up the folder, "I think you're going to find this interesting."

Lily smiled, "What did you find?"

"I had the wine bottle and the broken glass tested and it came back with the drug Colchicine. I knew that was a drug Beverly took off and on for swelling and pain in her knees. I believe someone put a very large amount into her wine."

Fergus and Lily looked at each other and then at Doc. Fergus rubbed his chin, "Interesting."

Lily leaned forward, "So she also had a large amount in her system. Is that so?"

"Yes, she did. An overdose of this medication will cause muscle weakness, among a host of other effects. With the amount that was in her system, she had to be feeling off. She may have experienced nausea along with stomach pain."

Fergus took in what Doc had just said, "From what I noticed out at the pool, her wine glass was broken by a chair. An empty bottle was under the nearby table, and Beverly was face down in the pool. She tried to stand, dropped her glass, stumbled, and fell into the pool".

Lily had a somber look on her face, "Wow! I hate to say it, but the Sheriff was right in saying she tripped and fell. However, he didn't look the scene over. I believe he and Beverly were more than friends. I think he was shocked to see it was her in the pool, and his emotions took over."

Doc Thompson closed the folder, "I'm going to send my findings over to the sheriff's office, and what he does with it, who knows?"

Lily stood up, "If he was having any kind of relationship with that woman, you would think he would investigate it as a homicide."

Kelly walked over, "You have to remember who we're talking about; Sheriff Sam doesn't like to work. He is here to wait out his retirement, and that is it. He called Blanche Smith's death a suicide, for god's sake!"

Fergus and Doc stood up. Fergus is showing no expression, "I'm retired, and this is out of Lily's jurisdiction."

Lily looked at Fergus, "Once a cop, always a cop. We're not done with this."

Fergus and Lily walked toward the door and stopped, "There have been three deaths at Sunshine Village. All three are considered a homicide by you, Doc. The Sheriff isn't investigating any of them. We have no authority here. Lil and I will nose around this weekend and see what we can come up with. It looks like we might have to call the state police on this one."

They said their goodbyes and headed back to Sunshine Village. In the car on the way back, Lily was watching the scenery, "Hey, what's your take on all of this with Beverly?"

"I'm not sure; she had a few different layers to her. She never exposed her relationship with the Sheriff. She may or may not oversee the windchime club. We know she has several clubs she was in charge of. I'm not quite sure what she was doing. I would like to get into her apartment and poke around."

"Her son is here; let's pay him a visit when we get back; invite him to have a drink." Lily smiled, "You know to loosen his lips." She said with a smile.

Fergus pulled into his parking space, "I like it; let's go see if he's available."

Beverly's apartment

Lily rang the doorbell. She could hear movement inside the apartment. A nice-looking man in his thirties answered the door, "Can I help you?"

Lily showed her badge and introduced Fergus as her retired partner, "May we come in?"

Oliver opened the door, "Come in, please. I'm Oliver."

"Nice to meet you, Oliver; thanks for seeing us on such short notice."

"I met Mr. Fergus earlier at the M.E.'s office."

Fergus looked around the room and noticed a couple of boxes, "We're sorry about your mother. We just came from the M.E.'s office. We were wondering if you would let us look around."

"Are you investigating her death?"

Lily walked over to the sliding glass door and looked out, "Yes, unofficially. Fergus is retired, and I'm out of the jurisdiction. However, we believe there is more to her death than meets the eye."

Oliver looked overwhelmed, "I just want to know what happened to her and why."

Fergus rubbed the back of his neck, "That is what we are trying to put together. Do you know any of your mother's friends?"

"I just met two little ladies with white hair from down the hall; they brought me over a casserole. They said they were sisters."

Lily walked by the boxes and noticed the pictures that were in them, "That was very nice of them. Did they say anything about your mom?"

"No, only that they were sorry and wanted to make sure I had something to eat."

"I see you have packed pictures; if you're like me, you have to stop and look at all of them before they go in the box."

"Yes, I've been taking a trip down memory lane."

"Are there any pictures of your mother and her friends from here?"

"I believe there are a few. They were in a small box that I just packed."

"Would you mind if we took them on loan?"

Oliver walked over to a box and pulled out a small blue box, and handed it to Lily.

Lily smiled graciously, "I'll get these back to you before you leave."

Fergus's eyes are still taking inventory of the room, "Would you mind if I look around?"

Oliver smiled, "No, go ahead."

Fergus walked into the bedroom; he opened the closet that was filled with clothes and shoes, all in order by color. The shoes were at the top of the closet in boxes with pictures of what was in each box stacked by heels, flats, sandals, and so on. He walked over to the bed and opened the nightstand by the bed; there was a book she had been reading, a pair of glasses, and a small flashlight. He then put his hand under the mattress and felt a book, he pulled it out, and it was a diary or ledger. He lifted the mattress and found another one. *Interesting, why would she keep these under the bed instead of in the nightstand?* He walked into the bathroom and didn't find anything out of the ordinary. He could hear Lily and Oliver talking from the other room. Fergus walked back into the kitchen area.

Lily looked up at him, "Find anything?"

Fergus stood with the books, "I did. Would you mind if I borrowed these? You'll get them back."

Oliver looked tired, "I don't care about the books. Maybe they will help with your investigation. I would like to have the pictures back."

Oliver turned as the buzzer on the stove went off, "My dinner, let me take this out."

"Sure, we will let you get to your dinner."

"Take whatever you need that will help with my mother's case. I don't know why someone would want to hurt her."

Lily handed Oliver her card, "Thanks, Oliver; we will show ourselves out. Call me if you think of anything that might help us or if you find anything interesting."

Oliver nodded. Fergus held up the books, "Thanks, it was nice seeing you again." The detectives walked back down to Fergus' apartment. Fergus set the blue box on the counter along with the two books he collected, "Let's go through this later. Are you hungry?"

"Famished!"

"Me too. Do you want to go back to that pizza place or eat here in the restaurant?"

"Why don't you call Cookie and see if she would like to join us? Let's go to that cute little pizza place. I want to get to know her better." Lily said with a smile.

Fergus smiled, "That's a wonderful idea."

'Mama and Pop's Pizza'

"Volare" by Bobby Rydell was playing inside Mama and Pop's. Lily and Cookie danced toward a booth where the three of them could sit comfortably. Cookie looked around, "I've seen this place from the road but have never been inside. This is wonderful. I love the décor. It makes one feel like they are in Italy. The music adds to the ambiance, don't you think?"

"I do, that is why I wanted to come back here. And for the food of course." Lily slid into the booth.

Menus were brought over by Mama herself, "Can I get you folks a nice bottle of wine?"

Fergus laid his menu down, "I am going to have a draft beer this time."

Lily put her menu on top of Fergus's, "Make that two."

Cookie handed Mama her menu, "I would like a glass of the house white wine."

Mama smiled, "What are we eating today?"

Fergus looked at the ladies, "Pizza?" They nodded in agreement.

"We would like the extra-large double meat supremo." He said with a smile.

Mama smiled, “Good choice; I’ll tell Pop to get that going for you.”

Mama returned with their drinks. Lily pulled out pictures she had taken out of the blue box. She laid them out on the table.

“Cookie, would you mind taking a look at these pictures and tell us who is in them?”

Cookie picked up the small stack of photos, “These look to be ladies that are in the clubs that Beverly was in charge of.” Cookie looked and found one with her friend Blanche; she held it for a few seconds, then passed the picture to Fergus, “This is my friend that lived in your apartment.”

Fergus held the photograph of a nice-looking woman holding a glass of wine. She looked like she was laughing. She had one hand holding her wine glass and the other up to her lips as she laughed. Fergus passed the photo back to Cookie. The look on Cookie’s face was evident that she missed her friend. “Blanche had an infectious laugh and personality. You would have liked her.”

Fergus put his hand on Cookie’s, “I’m sure I would have. I’m sorry you lost your friend.” Cookie smiled, “Thank you.” She looked through several pictures naming names when she came to a picture of the sisters. Fergus asked, “What can you tell me about these two?”

Cookie looked at the picture, “Well, they are sisters Hazel and Edna. They never married; at least, that is what I was told. I don’t know them personally, just to say hello in the hall.”She handed the picture to Fergus.

“Interesting.” Fergus held the picture. He looked up at Cookie, “I’m wondering why these two would be in a club that has an interest in single men when they didn’t seem interested in them in their earlier life. Why now?” He passed the picture back to Cookie. She looked at the photo and then up at Fergus, “I asked Blanche what they were up to. She told me they made several comments about not needing a man.

They enjoyed hearing the other women talking about the single men. I think it was more entertainment for them. If you stop and think about it, that probably gave them the thrill to hear all the juicy gossip."

Lily reached for the picture. She smiled, "These two look like grandmothers, very sweet looking. Fergie, aren't these the two we saw in the gym?"

"You're right, Lil, they are."

Cookie thumbed through the rest of the pictures telling who was who. Lily took mental notes. She placed the photos back into her purse.

Their pizza arrived at their table. The aroma of oregano, cheese, and Italian sausage filled their senses. Mama looked at the three of them, "Enjoy."

Fergus served the pizza on the plates and passed them to his left. "Don't be shy; eat up."

Conversation, laughter, and more pizza. Cookie was a comfortable fit; Lily and Fergus laughed at her stories. She shared some of the gossip at the village.

Cookie dabbed the corners of her mouth with her napkin, "Remember, this is gossip only. However, occasionally there will be some truth in there. I don't believe everything I hear and only half of what I see."

The pizza had disappeared when Mama came back to the table, "I see you are ready for dessert," she said with a wide smile.

Cookie shook her head no, but held her wine glass up, "I would like another glass, please."

Fergus looked at the dessert menu, "I would like to have the spumoni ice cream."

Lily nodded in agreement, "Make that two."

Mama looked at Cookie, “I’ll be back with your wine.”

Lily finished her beer, “I have really enjoyed coming to this place. We’ll have to make this a regular stop when I come to visit.”

Mama returned to the table with their ice cream and Cookies wine, “I’ll just leave this here.” She laid the check on the table.

Fergus placed his bank card on top. Mama smiled as she picked it up.

The conversation changed to the upcoming pool party. They talked about what they were going to wear and how the mood in the village had changed more to a positive note. Beer mugs and wine glasses were emptied.

Fergus patted his stomach, “I believe I’m filled up,” he said with a laugh. Lily and Cookie agreed. They waved at Mama on their way out, the same time that Mama called out, “See you next time.”

Chapter 22:
Bell Bottoms and Beer Let's Get Groovy!

It's the day of the pool party. Fergus was enjoying his morning coffee on the patio, watching as things were set up in the pool area. A banner is hung on the gate "Welcome to the 1960s."

Lily noticed Cookie in the hallway coming back from walking Lucy, "Good morning, Miss Cookie; how are you?"

"Wonderful, and you dear?"

"Fine, thanks for asking. I'm on my way for morning coffee with Fergie; why don't you join us?

"I'd love to," Cookie said with a smile as she unlocked her door, "What do you have there?"

"It's costumes for the party."

Cookie smiled, "Ooh, let me see." She peeked at what Lily was holding, "I can't wait to see Fergus all dressed up. This will be a whole different side of him."

"I made a coffee cake this morning; I'll bring it over."

"Yum, that sounds great; see you in a few."

Fergus heard his doorbell ring. He put his coffee cup onto the counter; he opened the door to Lily; her arms were filled with clothes.

"Here, let me take that for you." He reaches for the clothing.

"It's our costumes for today," Lily says with a broad smile, "Oh good, I see you have coffee on. I met Cookie in the hall. She will be here in a minute for coffee too."

Fergus smiled, taking the costumes into his bedroom, "Help yourself, Lil; you know where all my cups are."

"I'm one step ahead of you," she called out. Lily reached for two cups and then refilled Fergie's.

There was a knock at the door; Fergus opened it to see Cookie and her little poodle Lucy.

"You told me to bring her next time, so here we are." Fergus was glad to see them both. He pointed to the coffee cake, "What do you have there? It looks delicious."

"Cowboy cinnamon coffee cake." Cookie walked into the kitchen and set the cake down by Lily.

"Wow, Cookie, this looks and smells really good." She pulled a knife from the drawer to cut the cake.

Fergus picked up his coffee cup and leaned in to have a better look as Lily plated three slices, "I might have to have a couple of those; that is a thin slice, Lil."

"Oh, Fergie, I should have known." She cuts another small slice laying on top of the first and hands it to Fergus."

The three, including Lucy, go out onto the patio. Things were moving along quickly out by the pool. Cookie pointed out band members starting to set up. Tables were set up along the fence line, covered with tie-dyed table covers.

Fergus was almost finished with his coffee cake, "This is really good!"

Cookie blushed, "I'm glad you like it," she said with a shy smile.

The three watched the comings and goings out by the pool. The band was tuning their instruments; food was being set out. Cookie turned to Lily and Fergus, "I'm going to take Lucy home and get ready for this party." She picked up the empty plates as Lucy followed her to the kitchen. She turned toward Fergus, "Thanks for the coffee. I'll be back once I change and get Lucy settled in with a treat."

Fergus opened the door for her; he kissed Cookie on the cheek, "Thanks for the breakfast cake. Don't rush; come down when you're ready."

Cookie smiled as she turned to walk toward her apartment; little Lucy walked beside her.

Cookie stood in front of her closet; she pulled out the clothes she decided to wear. Lucy lay on the floor watching as Cookie changed. She put on a pair of faded blue jeans with wide bell bottoms and a boho green top with bell sleeves, "Well, Lucy, what do you think?" She walked over to the full-length mirror, checking out her outfit, "This should do." Cookie reached for a blonde wig she had on the top shelf in her closet. She pulled her hair up under a nylon cap and placed the wig on her head, styling it with her fingers as she placed a headband around her forehead. For the final touch, she put on three strands of love beads. Standing in front of the mirror, she looked down at Lucy, who tilted her head, "Well, how do I look?" Lucy gave a little bark as if to say; I like it.

Cookie smiled at Lucy, "Now you be a good girl. I'm going to go to a party just outside. You can watch from the patio window. Here's a treat; I'll be back in time to feed you." Lucy followed Cookie to the door giving her that look that always made Cookie feel guilty when she left without her.

Cookie locked her door and then walked down the hall toward apartment 110.

Fergus stepped back when he opened his door to Cookie in her hippie garb. She smiled at him, "Fergus, you look like Sonny Bono." She laughed, "Except he was much shorter."

"And you look like Angie Dickinson." He said with a smile.

Lily walked out dressed in hip-hugging bell-bottom jeans and a purple crop top. She had a long dark straight wig on. Cookie smiled at them dressed like a couple, "Sonny and Cher?" she asked.

Lily flipped her dark hair back behind her shoulder, biting her bottom lip, "Yep! I had these costumes picked out before I knew you were going to be Fergie's date."

Cookie checks the two of them out, "I think you two look cute!"

Lily was relieved at Cookie's reaction. They walked out through the patio to the pool area. Some residents were already seated at tables as the band began to play 60's favorites. Fergus found a table for the three of them. It didn't take long before food was cooking and drinks were being handed out. Several residents were dancing to the band.

Fergus and Lily were watching who was coming in, "Lookie Fergie, it's Gary Hart and he's with Lacy Martin. I wonder where Roxie is."

Gary waved at Fergus and Lily as he walked by their table.

"That's an interesting couple. I didn't know they knew each other."

Cookie leaned toward Fergus, "Remember, the singles here all know who is and isn't available."

Lily elbowed Fergie's arm, "Don't look now, but Sheriff Sam just walked in."

The band was playing "Magic Carpet Ride by Steppenwolf." Fergie stood up and reached for Cookie's hand, "Let's dance." Cookie smiled, "I'd love to."

Fergus looked at Lily, "See if you can engage our sheriff in some small talk." Lily nodded.

Sam, dressed in civilian clothes, walked toward Lily, "Hello Sheriff." Lily smiled as Sam looked at her trying to figure out who she was.

"It's me, Lily Bright, from Springfield."

"Ah yes, you threw me off with the long hair. Are you here for the party?"

"You know it. Are you here for the party, or is this an official visit?"

"No, this is my day off. I thought I'd stop by to see how things were going. Looks like everything is off to a good start."

"Have a seat; we have an extra chair."

Sam looked around at the dancers, "Great band." He sat next to Lily.

"Yes, they are good. Do you dance?"

Sam smiled, "Are you asking me?"

"Depends. Do you dance?"

Sam stood up, "Let's find out."

The two walked to the dance area when a slow song started to play. Sam pulled Lily close to him, "I can definitely slow dance."

Fergus and Cookie stayed out and noticed Sam and Lil on the dance floor.

Lily smiled, "Yes, you can. I'd say you're not half bad at it either."

Sam twirled Lily, "My mother taught me when I was in Jr. high school. She thought it would make me more sociable if I had dancing skills."

"And did it work?"

"I'd say yes, especially when the girls ended up dancing with each other because the boys were too shy to ask them to dance."

"Ah, I remember those days. I believe that still goes on today too. Girls seem to mature a little faster than boys at that age."

The song ended. Sam started to move back toward the seating area. Lily grabbed him by his arm.

"Not so fast. Let's see how well you dance to something more upbeat." The band started to play, 'Build me up Buttercup' by the Foundations.

Fergus and Cookie walked back to the table. Cookie leaned toward Fergus, "Lily seems to have our sheriff captivated," She said with a laugh.

"Lil will get him to feel comfortable, and hopefully, he might loosen up a bit."

Brian walked up to the table and sat down. Fergus and Cookie started to laugh.

Brian looked at them, "What?"

Fergus trying to control his laughter, "Did you not get the memo that this was a 60's party?"

"I did get the memo; however, I left the 60's clothes back in the '60s."

Lily and Sam walked back to the table. They both started to laugh.

"Brian, I didn't know we had pirates in the '60s," Lily said, trying to hold back her laughter.

Brian lifted the patch off his left eye, "This is the only costume I thought I would ever need moving here. Hey, at least I dressed up."

Sam moved a chair over from another table. The band continued to play old favorites and were taking a few requests. More residents were walking in. Brian was getting noticed. Several residents smiled as they walked by.

Fergus, Brian, and Sam walked over to the drink station that was handing out beer and wine.

Cookie scooted her chair closer to Lily, "Sam seems to be more fun out of uniform than when he's in uniform."

"Yes, I think he is feeling comfortable, which is good. Hopefully, he will open up a bit after he has a couple of beers."

The men carried red cups filled to the top with beer. Sam handed one to Lily. Brian held his cup up, "Cheers." Everyone else at the table held their cup and said "Cheers" in unison.

They sat at the perfect table to see who was coming in. Lacy walked in with a fellow Lily hadn't seen before, "Who's with Lacy?" She whispered. Cookie leaned toward Lily, "His name is Doug; he is a new single that just moved it. It doesn't take the women long to make a move on the newbies."

Lily stood up with a beer in hand, "I'm going to mingle a bit." She walked toward the back fence when she noticed the two little white-haired sisters. She walked up to them, smiling. Hazel poked her sister, "Look, Edna, it's Cher."

Edna looked Lily up and down, "I'll be darned! Are you going to sing for us?"

Lily laughed, "Not today. Are you two enjoying yourselves?"

"Oh yes, we love to come to parties."

Lily noticed the ladies didn't dress for the occasion, "No costume today?"

Edna shook her head. No, "we're not much for dressing up. We mostly like to people-watch. There is so much you can learn just by watching."

Lily watched the sisters thinking, *there is something about those two; I just can't put my finger on it,* "Well, you two enjoy yourselves." She turned and walked toward Gary, who was sitting with Lacey. "Hello, Gary, and Hello, Lacey."

Lacey looked surprised, "You two know each other?"

Lily smiled, "We do. We know each other from Springfield."

Gary swallowed as he looked at Lacey, "Ms. Bright investigated the death of my late wife."

Lacey sipped her wine as she watched the exchange between the two of them, "I see; I'm glad you were able to find who killed her."

"Thank you, we closed that case before Fergus moved here."

Gary looked uncomfortable. Lily noticed Eugene sitting alone by the fence, "Nice chatting with you two; enjoy yourselves."

Gary picked up a napkin from the table and wiped his forehead. Lacey looked concerned, “Are you okay?”

Gary smiled and patted her hand, “I’m fine. Seeing and talking to Ms. Bright just brought back memories that I’d soon forget.”

Lacey nudged Gary, “Let’s dance.”

Lily walked toward Eugene, and she smiled. Eugene smiled back. Eugene was sitting alone at a small table; he seemed to be enjoying the music.

“Mind if I join you for a few minutes?” Lily asked.

“No, have a seat.”

“Are you enjoying yourself?”

Eugene was doing what he usually does, watching people, “Why yes, I am. Things seem so much more settled since Beverly took a dip.”

Lily was surprised at the way he phrased Beverly’s demise, “So, I’ve been told. Have you noticed anything unusual since then?”

“No, not really. Like I just said, things are nice and quiet.”

“Let’s hope they stay that way. Well, take care. I just wanted to check in with you.”

Eugene waved at her as she walked away.

Lily walked back toward their table. She saw Sam get to his feet, “You’re not leaving, are you?”

Sam smiled at Lily, “If you’re going to twist my arm, I guess I could stay for a few more minutes.”

“Great! I want to visit with you for a bit. Tell me, where are you from originally?”

“Oregon, born and raised there.”

"What brought you here?"

"This job. I wanted to work in a small town. Get away from large cities. This came up, and I applied for the job."

"Interesting. Can you tell me about your relationship with Beverly? It seems like you two knew each other pretty well."

"We were just friends, according to her. I cared for her; she wasn't interested in a relationship."

"That's news. I knew she was hot on her heels for Fergie."

"Yes, I heard about that. She had hopes of getting married again. I was just a companion to her. She wanted more than I could give her."

"You felt differently about her, didn't you?"

"Yes, I loved her. I wanted to marry her. She turned me down every time I asked."

"I'm sorry, and I'm sorry for your loss. You know her death has been upgraded to a homicide, don't you?"

"Yes, I did get the notice from the M.E. 's office on that as well as Sondra's death."

"What is your take on all of this? I know you didn't initially think so."

"If the M.E. says it a homicide; then it's a homicide. I'll look at it as such."

"The death of Blanche is also suspicious; that is the one you called a suicide. Tell me you weren't seriously thinking that, were you?"

"I looked the scene over, and nothing looked out of place other than the dildo in the mouth."

"You know that dildo was shoved into that woman's throat, don't you? She wouldn't have done that."

"Look, this isn't a big city. I don't have the resources that you and your partner have had. There weren't any clues to follow on that one."

"Fergus and I have been looking at these deaths; if you would like to collaborate, we would be interested in assisting."

"I think we could do that." Sam emptied his red cup, "Ready for another?"

"Sure, why not."

She smiled.

Sam was warming up to the idea of working with Lily and Fergus. Which meant he would be the one in charge, and they could do all his footwork. He liked that idea; he would get all the credit for solving not one but two crimes.

Fergus and Cookie returned from the dance floor. Brian was dancing with one of the single ladies. The sisters danced with each other. Things started to wind down; residents started to head back to their apartments. The pool party was a success.

Chapter 23:
Am I a Suspect?

The following morning Lily walked down the hall toward Fergus's apartment, pulling her rolling suitcase behind her. It was early, and she knew Fergus would be up. When she rang the bell, she heard a dog bark.

Fergus answered the door with a smile. Lily could smell the coffee as she pulled her suitcase inside and parked it by the door, "I'm gonna need a cup of that coffee." She said with a smile. Little Lucy ran up to Lily to greet her, "Are you dog-sitting?" she asked as she petted Lucy on the head.

At that moment, Cookie walked out of the bedroom in Fergus' bathrobe, "Good morning." she said with a wide smile.

"Good morning, Miss Cookie." Lily looked at Fergus as he handed her a cup of hot coffee, "Sit, I made it just the way you like it." Lily reached for the cup, "I see the party continued after I left."

Cookie poured herself a cup of coffee. Fergus winked at Lily, "You could say that."

Cookie sliced the coffee cake from the previous morning out of the fridge. She handed a plate to Lily, "I think it tastes better on the second day."

"No need to feel awkward; we're all adults here." Cookie blushed; Fergus put his arm around Cookie's shoulder.

"I need to get back to Springfield sometime today. I was hoping we could run over some things from yesterday."

Fergus stood across from Lily at the counter, "Did our sheriff open up to you?"

"We did engage in conversation about his relationship with Beverly. He admitted they were friends with benefits. Apparently, his feelings for her were different than hers for him."

Fergus rubbed his chin, "Really?"

"Yes, he wanted to marry her. However, she had her eye on you. Her plan was to get married but not to the local Sheriff."

"I knew she had her sites locked in on me; she was very determined."

"To say the least!" Lily scoffed as she took a sip of her coffee.

"Beverly may have stumbled and fallen into the pool, a slip and fall as the Sheriff called it. We know someone tampered with her wine bottle. We also know that ninety percent of murders are committed by a family or their circle of friends."

Cookie placed a plate in front of Fergus, "Beverly was followed by many. There were only a few who didn't care for her. I don't know much about police work or how you catch a criminal. I do know who didn't like her."

"Fergus, do you have a notepad so we can make some notes?"

Fergus opened a drawer in the kitchen, pulled out a pad of paper and pen; he handed them to Lily.

Lily nodded to Cookie, "Give me some names."

Cookie sipped her coffee, "Well, there is me for one. Then you have Lacey, Roxanne, and Sondra. Don't forget Eugene; he blamed Beverly for his wife's suicide. Then there is Lizabeth."

"Sondra is dead, so we can't count her. Eugene, ah, I don't know. Of course, they always say it's usually the one you least suspect."

"Then don't forget our Sheriff; he could be a suspect. He admitted to you that he loved her, and those feelings weren't reciprocated. Rejection could have sent him over the edge."

Fergus sipped his coffee, "Cookie, you are right. We can't count the Sheriff out. Who is Lizabeth?"

Cookie smiled, "Oh, she is just a tiny thing that sits out by the pool most days getting her vitamin D. She will tell you. She is a bit absent-minded and single. I guess she used to work for a big title company up north. I have heard through the gossip pipeline that she was horrible at her job."

Fergus looked intrigued, "How so?"

"As I said, she was absent-minded; she would leave things out of contracts that would cause delays. Apparently, one of the higher-ups liked her. If you ask me, I think she was sleeping with him. She must have been good in bed to be able to retire with a pension."

Fergus almost choked on his coffee. Lily let out a laugh trying not to spit out her coffee cake.

"Cookie!" Fergus laughed, "You are too funny!"

"Fergus, I'm not trying to be funny. I'm just telling you what I heard and thought."

Lily walked over to the sink, setting her plate and cup inside, "Let's make the rounds today and see what we can come up with."

Cookie put the coffee cake back into the fridge, "I'm going to take Lucy home while you two do what you do best."

Cookie gathered her things; she put Lucy on her leash, "I'll see you two later for lunch?"

Lily smiled, "Yes, you will."

Fergus opened the door; he kissed Cookie on the forehead. She smiled, "Come on, Lucy, let's get you some food."

"We need to return these pictures to Oliver; we should start there."

Lily nodded in agreement. She placed her notes in her purse. Fergus locked his apartment. They walked the hall down toward the elevator.

Beverly's apartment

Oliver opened the door, "Come in. I was finishing up here; I need to get back home and back to work."

The partners walked in; Lily handed Oliver the blue box they borrowed, "We wanted to return these to you."

Oliver smiled, "Thanks, I appreciate that."

Lily looked around at the boxes he had packed, "You have been busy."

"Yes, I am having several boxes donated. I'm only taking a couple."

"What will you do with your mother's apartment?"

"I've been talking to the office, and I plan to put it on the market."

"Has anyone stopped by? Friends of your mothers that is?"

"No, just those two little ladies to pick up their casserole dish."

"Did they visit you?"

"They came in and had coffee with me, we chatted about my mother, and they told me how they enjoyed being around her. They shared a couple of stories."

Fergus looked intrigued, "Anything interesting?"

"Not really; they just talked about how she was in control of the clubs and how the ladies admired her. They talked about how popular she was. Hazel told me you were dating her, is that right?"

"No, I didn't date your mother. We had dinner together one evening. I was sitting alone, and she joined me. Well, thanks for lending us those pictures; we wish you well, and again, we're sorry for your loss." Fergus walked to the door. Lily patted Oliver on the shoulder, "Have a safe trip home."

As they waited for the elevator, Lily looked at Fergus, "I find it interesting that those two little ladies said they enjoyed being around Beverly. Popular? That woman was filled with venom. They fed him a bunch of bull crap. There is something about them that just doesn't sit right with me."

"Lil, maybe they just know things by watching like Eugene. I think they are just a couple of grandmotherly ladies that make it their business to know things. I also think they were trying to make Oliver feel better. Let's go pay them a little visit."

The dining room

Fergus and Lily walked the hall down by the restaurant and noticed Hazel and Edna seated in a nearby booth.

"Let's join them," Lily took the lead.

They walked up to the booth and the sisters smiled at them, "Good morning, Mr. Quimby and Miss Lily."

Lily slid in the booth beside Edna, “You don’t mind if we join you for a few minutes, do you?”

Fergus sat opposite Lily and Edna. Hazel moved over for him.

“We were just finishing up here; what can we do for you, fine folks?”

Fergus smiled at Hazel, “We just wanted to chat and see if you have noticed anything that might help with the investigation of Beverly and Sondra.”

Edna put her napkin on her plate, “I can’t say that we have, other than it’s been quiet lately. Sister, have you noticed anything that might help the detectives?”

Hazel smiled, “I wish I could tell you I have, but truthfully I haven’t noticed a thing.” She dabbed the corners of her mouth with her napkin, then laid it on the table.

Edna reached for her pocketbook, “Why don’t the two of you come up to our apartment where we can be more comfortable? The noise level is picking up in here.”

Lily got up, “We would love to; we just have a couple more questions; I’m sure you have the answers to.”

They walked toward the elevator; Edna pushed the button for the second floor, “One never knows what they might know or not. Maybe we can be of some help to you.”

Edna and Hazel’s apartment

As the sisters opened the door to their neatly kept apartment, Fergus found himself a seat on the couch. Lily walked to the sliding glass door and looked out over toward the pool area, “Nice view from up here.”

“Can we offer you a cup of tea or coffee?” Edna asked.

Fergus looked around the spacious apartment, "No, we've had our quota for this morning. How long have you two lived here?"

Lily walked toward the kitchen counter; she looked around the kitchen.

Hazel walked over to a side chair and sat down, "We moved in when they first opened. Isn't it a lovely place? One never gets bored here with all the activities."

Lily smiled as she turned toward Edna, who stood in the kitchen with her arms crossed, "Have you two noticed anything out of the ordinary going on around here?"

Edna uncrossed her arms, "I'm not sure what you mean."

"Suspicious; anything different than what would normally go on around here."

Edna looked at her sister Hazel, "No, I can't say that we have. We do enjoy watching people. Nothing that I can think of stands out. Hazel?"

Hazel nodded her head in agreement, "We're sorry we can't be of more help to you."

Lily looked at Edna, "What about Sondra?"

Edna crossed her arms again, "What about her?" she asked in return.

"Do you know anything about her death?"

Edna looked confused, "Am I a suspect?"

Hazel walked toward her sister, "Edna, don't ask such a silly question!"

Lily raised her eyebrows, "Should I think of you as a suspect?"

Edna grabbed her sister's arm, "I should hope not!, " she said in a curt tone.

Fergus got up and walked toward Lily, "Nice place, thanks for inviting us up. If by chance you do remember anything, please let us know."

Lily handed Hazel her card; she noticed she was missing a button on her blouse. Lily pointed to her blouse; "Do you know you're missing a button?"

Hazel looked down at her blouse, "You're right; I hadn't noticed. I'll have to fix that," she said with a smile.

Edna looked at her sister, "I think you should just toss it out; you've had that old thing forever."

Hazel smiled at the detective, "I have a hard time getting rid of things. You're right, sister. After today, it gets tossed."

The sisters walked behind them to the door, "We are happy to help." Edna said as she closed the front door behind them.

The dining room

Lily nudged Fergus as they walked to the elevator, "Did you notice the size of the button Hazel was missing?"

"I did, and I noticed they both have white hair. Lil, if you look around this place, over fifty percent of the residents here have white hair and wear clothing with buttons about that size. Besides, I don't think those two could pull something off like a murder. Let's see if we can run into Eugene."

"He's probably seated in his favorite watching place."

Fergus walked into the restaurant with Lily behind him; sure enough, Eugene was seated in the back, drinking coffee and reading the menu, "Good morning, Eugene; I thought we would stop by before I left. Did you enjoy the party yesterday?"

Eugene laid the menu down on the table, "Good morning, I had a nice time yesterday, thanks. Everyone else seemed to have a good time as well."

"Yes, it seemed that way. I know we enjoyed ourselves."

Fergus pointed to the chairs, "Do you mind if we sit for a minute?"

Eugene extended his hand toward the chairs, "Of course not, have a seat. Are you going to order something to eat?"

"No, we're planning on having an early lunch before Lily has to get back to Springfield. Did you happen to notice anything strange the day before Beverly was found in the pool?"

"No, nothing strange, just normal behavior with that woman."

"What do you call normal behavior for her?" Lily asked.

"She walked like she had a stick stuck up her ass that pushed her nose in the air. She gives an I'm better than you look to all the ladies in her clubs. She acts like she is doing them a favor to talk to them. I'd say that is her normal behavior. I can sum it up with one word, nasty."

Lily put her hand up to her mouth, trying not to crack a smile, "We know you didn't care much for her."

"How can you tell was it something I said? This place is quiet without her prancing around like a show pony."

"We have to ask; did you have anything to do with her death?"

Eugene smiled, "No, I did not; I would like to thank the person who finally put her out of her misery. When you find whoever it is, let me know and I will send them a card."

Fergus stood up, "Okay then, thanks for taking the time to talk with us; enjoy your meal."

Lily smiled, “Yes, thanks, Eugene.”

Eugene nodded as they walked toward the door.

Fergus’ apartment

Back in Fergus’ apartment, “Well Lil, who shall we pay a visit to next?”

“We haven’t talked to Roxie or Lacy, and I was thinking about stopping at the Sheriff’s office before I headed back to Springfield. What about Cookie?”

Fergus smirked, “Cookie didn’t kill anybody; she is harmless. I’ll check around and see if I can have a friendly chat with this elusive Lizabeth.”

“What do you think about talking with Madame Yvette again?”

Fergus raised his eyebrows and shrugged, “I haven’t really thought about it. What do you want to do, now have a séance?”

“What if it would help?”

“Lily! I’ve told you how I feel about this type of stuff.”

“You saw for yourself when she was here; we did get an answer to a question.”

“If that is something you want to do, you call her. I am not sure about all that hocus pocus stuff.”

“Good, I will call her.”

“Fergie, you can’t deny hearing the windchimes and the smell of perfume.”

“You have me there; I was a bit surprised. I am leaning in between believing and skeptic.”

“Maybe another session might make a believer out of you yet.”

The doorbell rang, and Fergus answered it to Lacey and Roxanne. Fergus smiled, “Lily and I were just talking about paying you two a visit. Come in.”

Lily stood up, “Hello, ladies.”

Lacy looked concerned, “We just saw a news brief about the homicides in our village!”

“Ladies, yes, we heard the M.E. has called the death of Sondra and Beverly a homicide. The Sheriff's office has been notified. In fact, we will be working with the Sheriff on this.”

“Oh good, we were afraid Sondra’s death would not be looked at because our Sheriff called it an accident.”

“Fergus and I know how upset you were with the death of your friend Sondra. What we would like to know is if you know anything about the death of Beverly. We know there was some bad blood between you.”

Lacey and Roxie looked at each other. Lacey asked with wide eyes, “You aren’t seriously looking at us as suspects in Beverly’s death, are you?”

Roxie scoffed, “I can’t say I’m sad she’s gone.” Lacey nodded in agreement.

Lily and Fergus watched the two women as they answered that question. Body language is important in an investigation. They noticed Lacey had her arms crossed, and Roxie wasn’t making eye contact, she would look down, and then her eyes would dart beyond the detectives.

Lacey brushed her hair behind her ears, “Are you finished grilling us? We came here to give you information, and you turn on us like we’re guilty of killing Beverly.”

Lily half smiled, “Lacey, we just asked a simple question; you’re the ones that are making this more than what it is. How well did you know Beverly?”

Lacey put her hands behind her back, “Well enough to know when she was being nice or fake nice.”

Fergus was intrigued by that answer, “Can you explain?”

“I could see it on her face. She had this look when she was being nice; there was a softness to her face; any other expression than that, I would know when she was up to something. They say the eyes are the windows to the soul; Beverly had no soul. We’re going to leave now unless you want to arrest us.”

Lily half smiled, “Ladies, please go on your way.”

Fergus opened the door for them, “Thanks for stopping by. After you’re done feeling offended by our question and think of something that might help us, you know where I live.”

Lacy turned on her heels, pushing Roxie in front of her toward the door, “Let’s get out of here.”

Fergus closed the door, “I wasn’t expecting that response.”

Lily laughed, “I knew what Lacy was talking about describing the facial expressions of Beverly. If you look back, we saw several of them.”

“I do believe I actually saw her nice expression.”

“Oh, come on, Fergie, I don’t think so; I think you saw her, I’m horny expression. I need to get back to Springfield.”

“What, no lunch?”

“I want to stop by the sheriff’s office before heading back.”

“Call me when you get home so I know you made it safely.”

Lily hugged Fergus, “I’m going to call Madame Yvette’ after I call you.” She smiled.

Fergus opened the door; Lily turned and smiled, “See you soon.”

Sheriff’s Office

Lily could see Sam sitting at his desk when she walked in. Sam looked to see who was in the office. He stood up and smiled, “Lily, come in.”

Lily smiled back, “Hey, I thought I would stop by on my way home.”

“I’m glad you did. What can I do for you?”

“I really enjoyed our chat yesterday at the party. There was one thing I forgot to ask you.”

“Okay, go ahead and ask. You have me intrigued.”

“Did you have anything to do with Beverly’s death?”

“You’re joking, right?”

“No, I’m dead serious. No pun intended. You yourself told me you were upset that she didn’t feel the same about you that you felt about her. You knew she was interested in Fergus. That had to hurt when she confirmed that to you.”

“Yes, I was hurt and disappointed she didn’t feel the same. I thought we had something special going on.”

“So, my question is, by her rejection did you snap and kill her? You know that old saying, if I can’t have you, then nobody can.” Lily stood in front of Sam, looking into his eyes.

“No, Lily. I did not kill Beverly; I loved her.”

"I had to ask. If the tables were turned, you would be asking the same questions."

Sam knew she was right; he was just surprised that she felt the need to ask him.

Lily walked toward the door; she stopped and turned, "Take care of yourself."

Sam waved her on, "Have a safe trip home."

"Yeah, thanks." Lily walked out of the office toward her car. Sam watched as she drove away.

Chapter 24:
"Sisters" By Irving Berlin

Edna and Hazel were singing the song "Sisters" as they were doing their Saturday chores.

"Sisters, sisters, there were never such devoted sisters, never had to have a chaperone, no sir, I'm here to keep my eye on her," they sang in unison.

Hazel danced around the apartment they shared with a feather duster for a microphone. Edna stopped in the middle of the kitchen with a broom, using it for a stand-up mic as they belted out the chorus, "Lord help the mister who comes between me and my sister and Lord help the sister who comes between me and my man."

They both broke into laughter.

Edna danced around in the kitchen, "Hazel, that's our theme song."

Hazel walked into the kitchen, still holding her feather duster mic, "We have a theme song?" The two sisters laughed until tears rolled from their eyes.

Hazel and Edna lived together in a modest apartment. Growing up with strict religious parents didn't prepare them for life in a world beyond that. The two were hard workers. They were careful with their earnings, only buying what was necessary and always paying their bills first.

Hazel was a secretary for an accounting corporation. Edna was a paralegal for a criminal attorney's office 'Justice Law Group'. They both made good money and were saving up for their futures. Both women had hopes of getting married, living in a beautiful home, and having a couple of children.

Edna, still holding the broom, looked at her sister, "Mom always used to say, 'cleanliness is next to godliness,' and let's not forget her favorite saying, 'House cleaning never killed anybody,' and you would say back to her, 'Not yet!' I remember you getting in trouble for that one."

Hazel smiled, "Yeah, I remember her smacking me a couple of times for being sassy."

"Ha! A couple of times? You always spoke your mind."

"Not always; otherwise, I wouldn't be standing here."

It was close to Christmas, and there was a chill in the air. Edna was late coming home from the office. Hazel was in the kitchen making soup and cornbread for dinner. The aroma from the kitchen hit Edna as she opened the door, "Smells wonderful, sister!" she called out from the living room.

"I was worried you weren't going to make it in time for dinner."

"I would have called if I was going to be any later. We had a busy day today."

Hazel filled two soup bowls with potato soup, "I couldn't do what you do all day. Working with people who have committed crimes and trying to get them off."

Edna sat down at the table as Hazel set her soup and cornbread in front of her. "Not all of them are guilty of what they are being accused of. I enjoy my job. I don't understand your job working with numbers all day; I think I would go blind doing that! However, something did happen today that I'm excited to share with you."

Hazel sat down across from Edna, "Tell me, tell me!" Hazel looked excited to hear Edna's news.

"You remember meeting my boss, Steve Greco."

"Isn't he the younger partner?"

"Yeess," Edna says slowly as she takes a sip of soup from her spoon.

"What about him?"

"Hazel, you outdid yourself this time." She takes another spoonful.

"Come on, sister, what is going on?"

"We have been seeing each other for about six months now. Just coffee and lunch when we have the time to get out of the office."

"Yes, you've told me about that."

"What I didn't tell you about is it's more than just a working relationship. Steve proposed to me today."

Hazel looked surprised, "you're getting married? I knew you had a working relationship. This is unexpected. I'm shocked! Why hadn't you shared this sooner?"

"You know I've had a secret crush on him since I've been working there."

"I know you have always talked about him. I know you always thought he would never be interested in someone like you; those were your words."

"Yes, those were my words. There was one day, we were in his office, and we were joking around. He asked a question unrelated to work, and I gave him a goofy answer. He stopped, and it was like he was seeing me for the first time. We looked at each other then he kissed me. Long story short."

"How come you never shared this with me?"

"I wasn't sure it would lead to anything. I never thought it would lead to a proposal! Isn't it exciting?" Edna was bursting with excitement.

Hazel laid her napkin in her lap, "I imagine it is for you; I'm still a bit shocked."

"Oh, sister, be happy for me."

"I am, really. Just give me a moment to absorb this news. Did he give you a ring?"

"We go to pick it out Saturday; then we'll go to dinner."

Hazel sipped her soup, "looks like we have a wedding to plan." Hazel said in a flat tone. She knew Steve from meeting him at events that she had been to with Edna. He was handsome and clean-cut; he always wore expensive suits. He was very hands-on with his employees. Pats on the back, hugs, very personable. She could see why her sister was drawn to him.

"Yes, Hazel, we do have a wedding to plan. Steve and I have agreed on a spring wedding. My heart has wings!" she said with a faraway look in her eyes.

Saturday

On Saturday, Edna met Steve downtown at 'Jewelry by Jean,' where Steve picked out a ring for his bride-to-be. "Oh, Steve, this is too much!" Steve laughed, "Edna, don't be silly. Nothing is too much for you." Edna's face lit up; she was so in love with Steve. The two hugged and kissed. Steve looked at the man behind the counter, "Sold!" Edna couldn't stop looking at her beautiful engagement ring, "Steve, I've never seen a diamond this big in person." Steve laughed, giving her a hug. As they walked out of the jewelry store, Steve turned Edna toward him, "I want you to follow me in your car." Edna had a quizzical look on her face, "Where are we going?" Steve walked toward his car, "Don't ask questions, or you will spoil the surprise." Edna did as she was told and followed Steve into 'Crown Mercedes's parking lot. Edna got out of her compact Toyota and walked toward Steve, "What are we doing here?" Steve pointed toward her old Toyota, "How would you like to continue driving that?" Then he pointed toward a new dark blue E320 Mercedes, "Or start driving that?" It had a huge red bow on the hood. Edna couldn't believe her eyes, "Are you kidding me?" Steve smiled as he looked into Edna's eyes, "I don't want my wife to be driving a Toyota, not that anything is wrong with a Toyota. I want you to drive in style." Edna looked shocked as she walked toward the Mercedes. Steve opened the driver's side door for her, "Get in, see how it feels." Edna slid into the driver's seat, "Oh Steve, it feels expensive." Just then, the salesman walked toward the car and handed Edna the car keys, "I think you will need these." Steve and the salesman shook hands. Edna looked at Steve, "What about my car?" Steve smiled, "The dealership will deliver it back to your house, and you can give it to Hazel, or we can sell it. Whatever you want to do." Edna didn't have to think about that, "Hazel would love to have my car."

New Year's Eve

New Year's Eve had arrived. The 'Justice Law Group' was having a party for their employees and family. Edna was excited; she pulled out a light blue mid-calf chiffon dress that was strapless from her closet.

Hazel didn't have a date and was going for her sister.

"Come on, Hazel; you'll have fun. There will be a few single men there; who knows, you might meet your future husband tonight."

Hazel stood in front of her closet, "I don't have anything to wear."

Edna walked toward the closet and pulled out a couple of nice dresses from Hazel's closet, "What's wrong with these?" She held up a red pencil dress with a sweetheart neckline and a green dress with a full chiffon skirt, "You look smashing in both. Pick one and quit pouting!"

Hazel walked toward Edna; she reached for the red one. "This will do." She said in a flat tone.

"For crying out loud, Hazel! You're acting like I'm making you go to a funeral! Snap out of it!"

She took her time getting dressed; standing in front of a full-length mirror, she smiled at how the red dress looked, "Not bad."

Edna looked out the window, "Hurry up, Hazel, the car is here." Hazel picked up her cape and pocketbook as she hurried toward the front door. They arrived at the senior partners' home. The town car drove down a long driveway to a huge two-story stately looking home. Hazel whispered to her sister, "Wow! I can't wait to go inside." Edna shushed her sister as she gave her a little nudge. The car stopped; a man in a suit opened their door. The sisters were directed toward the double front doors. Music could be heard as they walked up the steps. The doors opened to a large foyer that led to a staircase trimmed with green and red ball garland. Hazel was in awe as she looked up toward the staircase that led to the second floor. Edna elbowed her sister and whispered, "Hazel, stop gawking and close your mouth!" Hazel turned to her sister, "It's so beautiful."

Steve was standing in the foyer, holding a glass of champagne, talking with colleagues from the firm. They seemed to be having a good time. Edna walked up to Steve. He greeted her with a hug and a kiss on the cheek. Hazel decided to walk around and scope out the surroundings. Steve and Edna broke away to the dance floor. "You look beautiful, Edna." Steve pulled her close as they swayed to the music "White Christmas" Edna smiled, "You look pretty handsome yourself." The two danced cheek to cheek.

Hazel was taking everything in as she walked around with champagne in hand. The décor looked like it came out of a magazine. She was in awe. She made her way taking in each room on the first floor. The kitchen was buzzing with hors d'oeuvres being plated, champagne flutes being filled and taken out on trays. Hazel reached for another glass as a server walked by. She walked back through the living room. She saw Edna sipping champagne by a giant Christmas tree and talking to one of the secretaries from the office. The sisters made eye contact with each other. Edna smiled as Hazel walked back around toward the foyer. She stopped at the bottom of the staircase and looked up. She noticed Steve standing inside a doorway to one of the bedrooms.

A woman she had never seen before had her arms around his neck, and they were kissing. Hazel slowly backed away and made a beeline for her sister. Edna noticed the look on Hazel's face and knew instantly something was wrong, "Sister, is everything okay?" Hazel scoffed, "If you call Steve kissing another woman upstairs, okay, then I guess it is." Edna's expression changed from concerned to upset. Hazel followed her sister and watched as she slowly walked up the staircase. She stood at the bottom, trying to see what was going on. Edna said something to them; the music was loud. The woman in question pulled away from Steve. She brushed Edna as she rushed down the staircase toward the living room. Hazel couldn't hear what was going on due to the music that filled the home. However, she could see what was happening as Steve was slowly walking backward. It looked like he was trying to explain himself. Edna's face was red with anger as she pushed on his chest with both hands; lipstick was smeared on Steve's face. He slowly stepped back; his left foot lost its footing on the top step causing him to fall backward down the staircase. He landed at Hazel's feet. Hazel looked to the left and then to the right; she knelt by his head. No one was around; she looked up at her sister and then down at Steve as she grabbed the sides of his face. Steve didn't look good at all. Hazel jerked his head quickly to the left until she heard a snap. She laid his head gently down on the tile floor. Edna, halfway down the staircase, let out a scream as she rushed toward Steve. Hazel rushed toward the living room and called out, "HELP! SOMEONE, PLEASE HELP!" The music stopped, and a man called back, "WHAT'S HAPPENED?" Hazel turned toward the foyer and pointed, "HURRY, STEVE HAS FALLEN."

Edna was kneeling at Steve's side, holding his face in her hands, crying. A rush of partygoers gathered around Edna and Steve. Time seemed to slow down before the ambulance and police arrived. Steve was pronounced dead at the scene.

Edna and Hazel held onto each other in the car, taking them home. Edna looked at her engagement ring; she twirled it on her finger as tears streamed down her face. Her dreams were shattered; she felt lost. The new year hadn't arrived, and she was devastated.

Hazel and Edna's apartment

Once home, the sisters changed into their night clothes. Hazel did her best to console her sister, "Edna, he cheated on you right under your nose!"

Edna wiped tears from her eyes, "He told me Lana had been coming on to him."

"Who's Lana?"

"She's a new secretary Steve hired. I knew she was after him, the way she looked each time he spoke to her. Her big puppy dog eyes batted at him and laughed at things he said that weren't even funny. She always wore her clothes a little snug and her tops just low enough to make a man look."

"Didn't she know the two of you were engaged?"

"She knew alright; she didn't care. I asked Steve to fire her. He laughed at me and told me not to worry. He said he thought it was cute that I was jealous."

It's going to be okay; I know you're hurt now. I promise things will be okay."

Edna looked at her sister, "I saw what you did, sister; you snapped his neck! How could you? You didn't want us to get married, did you?"

"He was pretty much gone; his eyes were vacant. I just helped him. You didn't want him to suffer, did you? He would have been in a coma and probably never woke up. Would you want that? I don't think you would want to take care of a vegetable for the rest of your life. That is what he would have been."

Edna put her head down, twirling her engagement ring, "No, I wouldn't want him to suffer."

Hazel sat next to her sister on the bed. She put her arm around her shoulders, "Look, no one is ever going to hurt you again. No one loves you as much as I do. We have always looked out for each other since we were kids. Let's just think of this like Mother always would say, 'Keep your house clean, girls.' It's just house cleaning, sister, that's all."

"House Cleaning? Is that what we're going to call it?"

Hazel saw her sister was inconsolable, "Edna, get some sleep; we'll talk in the morning." She hugged her sister and kissed her forehead.

Edna pulled away from her sister. She put her hands up to her face as she cried uncontrollably. She lay down and finally went to sleep.

The following morning Hazel brought her sister a cup of coffee, "I made your favorite blueberry pancakes. Come have a few bites."

Edna shuffled in her slippers to the kitchen table, "I'm not hungry."

"You have to eat something; just take a couple of bites."

"I'd like to take a bite out of Lana; she caused this. If it wasn't for her, Steve would still be here. Why didn't he fire her when I asked him to? Sister, why?"

Hazel walked over to her sister, handing her the maple syrup, "Tell me about this, Lana."

Edna was able to eat a little bit as she filled Hazel in on Lana.

The funeral

Steve's funeral was two weeks later. It was a rainy day; friends and colleagues said their goodbyes. Lana stood close by, holding a single red rose. Edna's tear-stained face said it all; she was heartbroken. Lana walked up to the casket and laid the rose on top of the casket spray. She turned and walked away toward the parked cars. Hazel and Edna watched her as she left.

Steve had changed his will before Christmas. He left Edna everything, his share of the law firm, along with his home and personal effects. The first thing Edna did when she went back to work was fire Lana. Lana quietly packed up a box with her things and walked out without a word. It didn't bring Steve back, but it did feel good to get rid of the person who she felt ruined her life.

A month later

Edna and Hazel moved into the house that Steve had left her. As they settled in, Edna was still seething every time Lana's name came up. Hazel had had enough. She saw how this woman was tearing her sister up.

"Edna, do you know where this Lana lives?"

"I have her address at the office; why?"

"I think the only thing that is going to make you feel better is if we do a little house cleaning."

Edna had a surge of excitement rush through her body when her sister brought that up. "What do you have planned?"

"I'm working on it. Bring her address home after work, and we can talk about the details."

Edna smiled at her sister, "Done!"

The following Monday, Edna brought Lana's personnel file home with her. Hazel looked it over. The sisters took a drive to see if she still lived at the same address. They parked on the street across from her house in Hazels Toyota. The curtains were open when they saw Lana walk by a window; Hazel smiled at her sister, "Perfect! House Cleaning starts tonight."

The sisters went home. They were dressed in dark clothing. Hazel put together what she called her cleaning supplies. It was midnight when they drove back to Lana's house. The lights were off. They parked on the side street and walked toward the backyard. They carefully walked toward the back slider off the patio, not stepping in planter areas, only onto grass and concrete. Edna reached for the slider door handle; it was locked. Hazel motioned to her sister and pointed to the back door of the garage; she whispered, "Let's give it a try." It was unlocked. As they entered, the window in the garage provided just enough light for them to see the door to the house. Hazel turned the handle, and it opened. She smiled at her sister, "See, sister, everything is going our way. This is meant to be." The two tiptoed through the kitchen toward the bedroom. Hazel could see Lana lying in her bed asleep. In the hallway she opened her cleaning kit. She pulled out a vial of insulin, opened up the syringe, and filled it. She handed the cleaning kit to Edna to hold. Hazel tiptoed to Lana's bedside and injected the insulin into her neck. Lana opened her eyes and sat up. Hazel backed away, "Don't worry, Lana, I'm just the cleaning lady." Lana grabbed her neck and laid back down. Hazel walked out as Edna followed her through the kitchen and out of the garage. There were no sounds from inside. They got back into the Toyota and drove home. Edna felt relieved. Hazel smiled at her sister, "See, sister, a little housecleaning can make you feel better."

Edna dated off and on throughout the years. No one compared to Steve; no one ever would. Hazel never married; she stood by her sister's side. They were attractive enough. They decided to have fun and stay single.

When Edna retired, she sold her share of the law group to one of the partners. She also sold her home. The sisters moved together to Sunset Village, where they bought the largest apartment that was available. Hazel was always there for her sister. They had a pact since childhood. No matter what, they would be there for one another. If anyone got in the way, they would just do a little bit of house cleaning.

Chapter 25:
"Stray Cat Strut" by the Stray Cats

Even though the pool party seemed like a success with the residents, rumors were still swirling throughout the complex about a serial killer on the loose.

The graffiti was cleaned off the driveway. However, you could still make out the message, 'Move in and die.'

Several residents had moved out, put up their condos for sale or rent. This was good for Roxie; she had high hopes of purchasing Sondra's apartment at a reduced rate.

Roxie received a call from Malissa at the front desk, "Hi Malissa, have you come up with a price for Sondra's condo?

"I'm calling you to let you know we received a cash offer on that unit that we accepted. I know you were very interested. That offer was more than what we were expecting to get at this time. I know you must be very disappointed. I am sorry. You know the saying "cash talks."

"Why didn't you contact me? I would have liked the opportunity to counteroffer?"

"With the way things have slowed down here, prices have drastically dropped. Besides, it wasn't up to me; it was up to management. They made the final decision. I hope you can understand our dilemma."

"NO! I don't understand! Yes, I'm very disappointed. Thanks for nothing, Malissa!"

Roxie slammed the phone down. Trying to compose herself, she goes out to the pool to meet up with Lacey.

Lacey saved a seat next to hers. There were wine coolers on ice in a portable cooler. Lacey noticed the look on Roxie's face as she walked over to the lounge chairs, "What's wrong? I can tell when you're upset. Spill it, girlfriend."

Roxie sat down; she reached for a cooler, "I don't think I can talk about it right now."

"I'm so sorry you're upset. I happen to have some good news that might cheer you up."

"I don't think so, but go ahead anyway." Roxie sipped her wine cooler as she looked toward Lacey.

"With all the craziness that is going on here, I heard through the grapevine that prices have dropped. Our condos have decreased in value."

Lacey brushed her hair back and tied it with a scrunchy, "So I've been told."

"With that knowledge, I decided to take advantage of the situation. You know I've been renting since I moved here. My lease will be up at the end of this month."

"You're finally going to buy?"

"Yes! I'm so excited."

"That is good news; I'll drink to that! I'm so happy for you, Lacey."

"I have already made the purchase. It's not just any old condo."

Roxie held up her wine cooler in the air as she looked at Lacey, "Cheers! I hope you will be close to my unit."

"As a matter of fact, I will be across from you, well almost." She said with a smile.

"That is great. What's the number?"

With excitement in her voice, she blurted out, "114."

"114? What the hell? That is Sondra's condo!"

"Yes! I purchased it with everything in it! Can you believe it? I was so surprised when my offer was accepted."

"SO, YOU'RE THE ONE!" Roxie shouted at Lacey. Others at the pool looked in their direction.

"What! I don't understand why you're so upset. I thought you would be happy for me."

Roxanne glared at Lacey as she said with gritted teeth, "I was working with Malissa on purchasing that unit! You took that right from under my nose!"

"How was I supposed to know that you had made an offer on that unit? You never mentioned anything about wanting to purchase it. Just how in the hell am I supposed to know what goes on in that pea brain of yours? Huh?"

Roxie stood up, staring at Lacey, "HOW COULD YOU!"

Her face turned red with anger.

"DON'T YOU GO ALL CRAZY ON ME BITCH! YOU ALREADY HAVE A CONDO! I'VE BEEN RENTING. YOU KNEW I WANTED TO BUY WHEN THE MARKET CHANGED.

PRICES CAME DOWN, AND I WAS ABLE TO TAKE ADVANTAGE OF THEM.

Roxie was so furious she poured her wine cooler on Lacey. Lacey stood up, dripping with red wine, and shoved Roxie, "YOU BITCH! WHAT IS WRONG WITH YOU?"

"YOU'RE CALLING ME A BITCH?" Roxie shoved Lacey back. People were watching the commotion that was going on. Lacey moved toward Roxie, pushing on her until she fell backward into the pool. Lacey then threw her wine cooler can at her; it nearly hit Roxie in the head, "I WANT THOSE SHOES BACK THAT YOU BORROWED FROM THAT CONDO!" She grabbed her stuff and stormed out of the gate.

Roxie got out of the pool, dripping wet. People were still staring, "WHAT IS YOUR PROBLEM? DON'T YOU HAVE ANYTHING BETTER TO DO?" Everyone turned away except for Eugene, who watched with interest. Roxie grabbed her things and strutted toward the gate. She stomped off toward her condo.

Fergus watched the commotion from his patio. The sisters watched from their apartment that faced the pool area.

Fergus' phone rang, "Fergus here."

"Fergie, I wanted to let you know that I made it back to Springfield in one piece."

"Thanks for calling; I'm glad you made the trip safely."

"Anything good happened since I left?" Lily said with a chuckle.

"As a matter of fact, yes," I just watched a blowup between Roxanne and Lacey out by the pool."

"Really?" Lily said with interest, "I thought they were besties."

"I think that ship sailed."

"Did you happen to hear what it was about?"

"Oh yes, it has to do with Sondra's condo. Apparently, they were both interested in purchasing it without telling each other, and Lacey got the jump on it."

"Interesting! So, there was a catfight, huh?"

"And a good one at that, fighting like a couple of stray cats. Lacey shoved Roxie into the pool and threw her wine cooler can at her head. That lady and I say that loosely has an arm on her. It almost hit Roxie in the head." Fergus laughed.

Lily laughed along with Fergie, "I'm sorry to have missed that.

"It happened quickly. There was an audience. I noticed Eugene taking it all in."

"I'm not surprised he seems to be watching everyone. Remember, Brian calls him the watcher."

"Never a dull moment here, it seems. I'm going to check around and see if I can find out who Lizabeth is and have a chat with her."

"Did you ever find out who was watching from the balcony the night Beverly fell in?"

"No, not yet. That is on my list of things to do. I will keep you posted. How did your visit go with our Sheriff as you were leaving town?"

"He acted a bit surprised that I asked him if he killed Beverly. I don't think he had anything to do with it. However, he knew I had to ask the question."

"I hope he is doing something on his end and not expecting us to do all his work for him. I get the feeling that is what he is up to."

"I wouldn't be surprised if that is exactly what he is up to. We have both heard how he is just biding his time until he can retire. I've got to get to the station. I'm going to run a background check on our two feisty grandmothers along with Eugene. I think while I'm at it, I will check on Lacey and Roxanne too."

"Okay, let me know what you come up with, if anything. I'll talk to you soon."

"Later, gator."

Chapter 26:
Andrea Day Reporting

Andrea Day arrived early at her desk. It was covered in post-it notes of the possible story leads. She noticed a letter that wasn't there when she left the night before. The postmark was local. There wasn't a return address. She sat down, wondering who it could be from. Holding the letter, she opened it carefully. It was neatly typed with all capital letters on a purple piece of paper.

ANDREA DAY,

ARE YOU GIVING UP? DON'T YOU CARE THAT THERE IS A SERIAL KILLER ON THE LOOSE IN SUMMERS BAY? THERE HAVE BEEN THREE DEATHS ALREADY BLANCHE SMITH, SONDRA MILLER, AND BEVERLY JOHNSON. WHO WILL BE NEXT?

CONCERNED CITIZEN

Andrea held onto the letter. She looked around the newsroom; Stewart was seated at his desk. Andrea stood up and called out, "Stewart, come take a look at this." She waved the letter back and forth.

Stewart looked like he just got out of bed. He took his time walking to her desk. Andrea looked him up and down, "late night?"

He yawned, "You could say that I have a new puppy. She cried most of the night."

"Aww, so you're a new dad, how cute." she smiled, "Now try to shake it off and check out this letter. It was sitting on my desk when I arrived this morning."

She handed the letter to Stewart, and as he read it, he raised his eyebrows. He handed it back to her, "I take it, we're going back to Summers Bay?"

"Yep! You got that right. The killer may have sent this!"

"What makes you think that?" He yawned again.

"Because it was sent with no return address, it was typed and was signed, concerned citizen. Criminals do this kind of crap! That is what makes me think that! Now get your camera and let's get a move on; we have a story to report."

Stuart and Andrea arrived at Sunshine Village. "Come on, Stuart, I've seen snails move faster than you," Andrea begged.

She poised herself in front of the complex as she waited for Stuart to start filming. He gave her the signal he was rolling.

"This is Andrea Day reporting from Sunshine Village in Summers Bay. I'm standing in front where there have been three deaths reported in the past few weeks." She walked toward the driveway and pointed down, "If you look closely, you can still see the faint paint that read, 'Move in and die.' Rumor has it a serial killer is living in this complex. Residents are frightened. If you look toward the side of the building, you will notice a couple of moving trucks. Residents are moving out." She motioned for Stewart to stop filming.

Stewart followed Andrea toward the front doors, "Be ready to roll when I give you the signal."

Malissa stood from behind the front desk, "Hold it right there! Where do you think you're going?"

She motioned for Stuart to start filming. "Ma'am, we're from WXLA News. There is a story here, and I'm going to report it." Andrea walked past the front desk, followed by her cameraman.

Malissa's mouth was open, "I'm going to ask you to leave now."

Andrea continued down the hall toward the door, going out into the courtyard by the pool.

Malissa walked back to her office with a smile; the wheels were in motion.

Fergus was sitting on his patio when he saw the news people were back. Andrea spotted him right away.

"Detective Quimby, can I ask you a couple of questions?" she said with her television smile.

Fergus rubbed his neck, "You can ask; I may not be able to answer. For the record, I'm retired."

The camera is still rolling, "Mr. Quimby are you working with Sheriff Sam on the deaths that have taken place here?"

"The sheriff and I have talked. However, he is the man in charge. This is his jurisdiction. Remember, I'm retired."

"Yes, sir, I remember. Once a detective, you don't stop when something like this falls into your lap, do you? Look at the view you have of this beautiful pool area. Surely you saw what happened to Beverly Johnson."

"I was in bed asleep when Ms. Johnson lost her life. According to the Medical Examiner, he said she drowned. You might want to talk to him."

"What do you know about Sondra Miller? She was murdered in her own apartment, isn't that so?"

"Again, that is what the Medical Examiner's Office said."

"Blanche Smith, was that murder too?"

"According to the Medical Examiner's Office, that was natural causes."

"Come on, detective, I know you know more than you're saying. Throw me a bone, will ya? I received a letter typed on purple paper stating that there was a serial killer on the loose here. What are your thoughts on that?"

"Like you, I've heard the rumors, and that is what they are, just rumors."

"Mr. Quimby, sometimes rumors turn into truths."

Fergus stood as he opened his patio door. He turned toward Andrea and her camera. "So, I've been told. Nice chatting with you. Have a good day."

Andrea motioned for Stuart to follow her toward the pool area, "This is where the third death occurred. It had been called an accident. Residents have their own ideas." She pointed to Fergus' apartment, "The apartment that Mr. Quimby now resides in is where the first death occurred. Blanche Smith's death has been called natural. What is natural when the body is found with a dildo shoved down her throat? Sheriff Sam called it suicide, really sheriff?"

The second death was in unit 114, the home of Sondra Miller, who was found by her friends with a stiletto shoved deep into her eye socket. That death was called a household accident by, guess who? Sheriff Sam. The Medical Examiners' Office has called that death murder. My question is, are all three of these deaths related? Andrea Day reporting from Sunshine Village in Summer's Bay for Wxla News. She motioned to Stewart, "THAT's a wrap! Let's pack it in."

Andrea smiled as she walked by the front desk, "Be sure to watch the five O'clock news."

Sunshine Village was the first story that ran at five O'clock. Malissa watched and knew this was going to be horrible for business, or was it? Many residents had given notice that they were selling. Renters were giving notice as well.

Rumors ran wild around the village. Residents wondered why those women were targeted. Was someone else going to end up dead? Then the big question arose is management trying to cover up what is happening? Is there a serial killer among them?

Chapter 27:
The Color Purple

After Andrea Day's newscast aired, management decided to take a stand. Flyers were made up and sent out to all residents.

Windchime Club Members

It has been brought to our attention that this is a club in our village. This is not a recognized club; it is not an official charter club. We ask those of you who are partaking or members of this club to remove your purple windchimes due to recent events that have taken place here. This club must be disbanded immediately. We thank you for your cooperation on this matter. If you have any questions, you may contact management.

Sunshine Village Management

Cookie took the flyer over to Fergus' apartment, and Lucy followed closely behind her.

Fergus was happy to see that it was Cookie on the other side of his door, "Come in; I was just thinking about you."

"Ooh, I'm flattered." She said with a smile in her voice as they hugged.

“Have you received one of these flyers yet? She held up the flyer printed on light violet paper.

“Yes, it’s about time management acknowledged that this club even existed. I happened to be on my patio when the news station came by to report on the recent deaths here.”

“Yes, I saw that newscast. Something more to upset residents.”

“The interesting thing is that the news lady said she received a letter typed on purple paper. That makes me think that it was sent from here.”

Cookie looked surprised, “You think someone from the office sent that letter?”

“I do.”

Lucy was excited to see Fergus. She greeted him, and then she was off doing what she does best, running around the apartment and exploring each and every room.

“Come in, have a seat. What can I get you to drink?”

“Water would be great.”

Fergus set a bottle of water in front of her. His phone rang, “let me get this. It’s Lily.”

“Sure, take your time.”

“Hey, Lil, what’s up?”

“Does Cookie happen to be there by any chance?”

“As a matter of fact, she is sitting here with me now. She just came over with Lucy.”

“Would you please put me on speaker? She needs to hear this as well.”

“Sure, just a second. Ok, I’ve got you on.”

"Hi, Cookie. Can you hear me?"

"Yes, I can hear you. What's going on?"

"I just got off the phone with Madame Yvette. You're not going to believe this. Here goes. I called her to see if we could get her to come back over. She told me there was no need. She had a vision-like dream where Blanche appeared to her. She claimed that Blanche has a message for you, Cookie."

"What's the message?" Cookie leaned forward as if she would be able to hear better.

"She said Blanche wants you, Cookie, to go to her apartment. Fergus' apartment now. She said there was a clue there. She kept saying "Tell Cookie, tell her."

Fergus interjected, "Interesting. I can guarantee you there is nothing here to be found."

"She also said to tell Cookie nothing could have been done to stop what happened to her. It was her fate. She is with her husband now."

"Thanks, Lily, for calling her; I really appreciate you for doing that." Cookie leaned back on her stool.

"My pleasure Cookie; let me know if you two come up with anything interesting."

"I don't think that is going to happen. This place was gone over before I moved in, and I haven't seen or found anything since I've been here. As you know, it's not a very big place."

"I'm just the messenger, Fergie. Anyway, I'll let you two go and will see you soon."

Fergus and Cookie said in unison, "Bye, Lily."

Fergus set his phone back on the counter. Cookie looked around and didn't see Lucy.

"Lucy!" She called out to her, "You come here."

Fergus smiled, "She can't hurt anything. Let her explore."

Cookie laughed, "She explores every time we come over here. You would think she has it down by now."

She was in Fergus' bedroom. She has been in there quite a while.

"Lucy, what are you up to? You come to Mama now." she said sternly.

Cookie walked toward the bedroom, "Oh no! I think she has something I can hear her digging. I better check."

Fergus followed closely behind Cookie. Lucy was in the closet. She was in the back left corner digging at the floor.

"Lucy! You come out of there." Cookie called. Lucy continued digging in the back of the closet. When Cookie reached in to pull her out, Lucy bared her teeth and growled at her.

"Lucy! You don't do that to your Mama."

Fergus, surprised at Lucy. He wondered what she was doing in the corner of his closet. He picked up a flashlight off his nightstand, "Hey girl." He patted her on the head, "What are you doing in there?" He shined the light toward the corner and noticed an ink pen. He reached toward the back and picked it up. "What do we have here?"

Cookie leaned in toward Fergus to have a look, "That must have fallen out of your jacket pocket or pants when you hung them up."

Fergus nodded his head, "Maybe." He took a closer look at the pen. It had the letters E. W. printed on it. "This isn't my pen. No one has been over here with those initials that I know of. Could this belong to Blanche? Could this be what she was trying to tell us about?"

Cookie looked at the pen, "Those aren't Blanche's initials or her husband's."

Fergus holds the pen up, "Interesting." He took the pen into the kitchen and put it in a sandwich bag.

Cookie looked confused, "Why are you doing that?"

"Because, my dear, this might be something that was overlooked and could possibly be a clue to Blanche's visitor on that fateful night."

"Wow! I bet this is what Blanche meant in her message. How could that have been missed?"

"It's a black pen with white initials in the far back corner of the closet; I can see how it could have been missed."

Fergus patted Lucy on the head, "Good girl! You might make detective, yet."

Cookie laughed, "I was worried she was being naughty, and instead, she uncovered a possible clue."

Cookie carried Lucy back into the kitchen area and put her down, "You be a good girl and go lay down." She reached for her water bottle, "What are your plans for the rest of the day?"

"I'm going to see if I can find out who was on the balcony when Beverly was in the pool, and I want to locate Lizabeth."

"Lizabeth won't be hard to find. Check out the beauty shop or the nail salon. If she isn't there, she might be in a meeting. She is president of the karaoke club."

"Sounds like another Beverly," Fergus said under his breath.

"Close but not as bad. Lizabeth has a strong personality. Beverly didn't like her at all. I'm sure the feeling was mutual with Lizabeth."

"How will I recognize her?"

"She is a small lady five feet tall, if that. She might weigh about one hundred pounds. She had her dark brown hair always in a French twist. Her voice is very distinct. She has what we call a Western accent or cowboy accent. She lived on the west coast before moving up north, and then she retired here."

"Do you know her personally?"

"No, just in passing. I don't know if you know this or not. When someone new moves in here, there is always a little write-up on them in our bulletin. How do you think all those single ladies found out about you?"

Fergus smiled, "I never thought about it."

"Blanche knew her from the karaoke club."

"So, Blanche was also a singer?"

Cookie smiled, "She tried; it was something she always wanted to do. Don't get me wrong; she could carry a tune; however, it wasn't always in tune." Cookie smiled as she remembered her friend, "I used to go with her and watch her perform."

"Is there anything else I should know about this, Lizabeth?"

"She wasn't in any of Beverly's clubs because Beverly was in them." She laughed. "Who knows, she might take them over now that Beverly is gone."

Fergus put his empty coffee cup in the sink, "I'm going to check around and see if I can come up with anything. You're welcome to stay."

"I'm going to clean up and head back to my apartment with Lucy. Happy hunting."

Fergus walked into the nail salon, and sure enough, from the description Cookie gave, he found who he was looking for. She was seated in a big chair, soaking her feet. A technician was giving her a pedicure.

A lady behind a desk called, "Sir, do you have an appointment?"

"No, I don't. I want to chat with this young lady for a moment."

Lizabeth looked up at Fergus, "I know who you are." She said with a wide smile.

"Great! Mind if we chat for a minute?"

"I'm all yours, what's on your mind?"

"Beverly Johnson."

"Oh her! Can't we talk about anything other than her? That woman was nothing more than a pain in my ass!"

"That is what I've heard. I've also heard you're not the only one that felt that way."

"Bossy bitch that is what I know about her. She thought she was better than anyone else and could do no wrong. I was glad to hear she was gone. I don't have to pass her in the hall or see her anywhere in this complex ever again."

"I take it you two didn't socialize?"

"What was your first clue?"

"Do you know who would want her dead?"

Lizabeth laughed, “You’re kidding, right? Just about every woman in this complex and a few men.”

“What about you? Did you want her dead?”

Lizabeth smiled, “I may have wished her dead a few times; I might even have dreamed of knocking her off myself. If you’re asking if I was involved in her death, the answer is no.”

“What about Sondra Miller? Were you friends?”

“We were friendly. Sondra didn’t put up with Beverly’s crap either. Oh, you can’t ask her, can you? That is probably because Beverly killed her. She threatened to do that in the restaurant in front of everyone.”

“Maybe she did, maybe not. That is an open case. What about Blanche Smith?”

“She was a nice lady. She got involved with the wrong group, and that was the beginning of the end for her.”

“Do you know who might have visited her that night?”

“I haven’t heard anyone talk about that. If I had to guess, she met up with someone in that club who had other ideas than what it was formed for.

“From what I’ve heard, that windchime club was quite popular.”

“It was popular with many of single women. In case you haven’t noticed, more women are here than men. There have been more STDs associated with that club than you find in a local high school.”

“How do you know all this?”

“People talk, especially women.” She said with a snide laugh.

“Thanks for chatting with me. Take care.”

"Hey, come by the karaoke club tonight, and you might enjoy yourself. Sing, dance, and meet some very nice people."

"Maybe I will." Fergus waved to the lady behind the front desk as he exited the nail salon.

Fergus walked up to the front desk; he tapped the bell on the counter. Malissa left her office, "Fergus, what can I do for you?"

"Can you tell me who lives in apartment 235, which overlooks the pool?"

"Let me check." Malissa walked into her office and checked on her computer. "I sold that condo a couple of months back to Doug Howard. He just moved in recently. Is there a problem?"

"No, no problem. Thanks."

"Happy to help, have a good day."

Fergus waved as he walked toward the elevator.

Doug Howards apartment

Doug was having toast with his morning coffee when his doorbell rang. "Give me a minute," he called out, reaching for his bathrobe behind the bathroom door.

Fergus smiled when the door was opened, "Hey, sorry to bother you. I didn't get you at a bad time, did I?"

"Oh no, I was just having my morning coffee. What is it I can do for you?"

"Let me introduce myself; I'm Fergus Quimby, a retired homicide detective. I live on the first floor."

"Nice to meet you, Fergus; I think I've seen you around. I'm Doug Howard. Won't you come in?"

"Just for a minute; I won't take up much of your time." Fergus noticed the apartment was decorated, and it looked like Doug had lived there longer than Malissa had told him, "I heard you just moved in."

"Yes, however, I bought it a couple of months ago. I only came over on my days off from work. I wanted to be settled before I retired."

"No wonder it looks like you have been here longer. I've seen you in the restaurant dining with Roxie and Lacey a few times."

"Yes, very nice ladies. They make good company."

"What is it I can do for you, Fergus?"

"I noticed you on the balcony the morning Beverly Johnson was discovered in the pool."

"Yes, I stayed over that night. I was unpacking the last of my boxes the night before. I went out on the balcony to have a cigarette."

Did you see anyone out by the pool at that time?

"No, I can't say that I did. Like I said, I just went out to have a smoke. Around midnight I heard someone calling out your name. It woke me up; I got up to check what was happening. I noticed a woman out there in her nightgown; she looked drunk. I closed my slider and tried to ignore her to get some sleep. The following morning, I saw her floating in the pool. You and a few others were already out there."

"She was calling my name?"

"Yes, I'm surprised you didn't hear her. Was she murdered? I've heard all the rumors."

"The Medical Examiner's Office believes there is foul play. I appreciate you taking the time to chat with me."

"Sure, anything I can do to help. I'll probably be seeing you around."

"I'm sure you will; thanks again, Doug."

Chapter 28:
Dear Diary

Fergus walked into his apartment. Cookie had washed his dishes and left him a note. *Meet me for lunch at the bistro, hugs, Cookie.* Fergus smiled as he laid the note back onto the counter. He walked into his bedroom remembering the two diaries he brought back from Beverly's. Since Oliver didn't want them back there wasn't a big hurry to go through them sooner. He carried them to the kitchen counter. He grabbed a tablet and pen to take notes as he thumbed through them. Most of what he saw in the first one was planning for the clubs she wanted to start. People she met, what she thought about them. She was just as brutal in her writings as she was in public. Fergus thought to himself, *this woman has no filter. It didn't matter to her who she hurt.* He picked up the second diary. It had much more detail than the first one. She wrote about things she wanted to have happen, things she made happen and people especially women she wanted to get even with. There was a list of names with check marks by some, stars by others, along with doodles she made on the side of the page. He found the list of single men and notes by each one. *Interesting,* he thought as he turned the page and saw a paragraph about himself.

A new single man just moved into Blanche's old condo. I hear he is a retired detective. He sounds yummy! I was able to get a look at him from a distance. I think I'm in love. It shouldn't take very long to make him mine. I'll be making a drive to Ocean City to pick up an apple pie made from scratch by Candy's Sweet Shop. I will be putting the ladies on notice that he is off limits. They will comply if they know what is good for them.

Fergus shook his head as he read on, "Beverly, you were a piece of work!"

Today I met my detective. I delivered the apple pie to him. I think he bought it when I told him I made it. It was made from scratch. I just didn't do it, ha, ha. I was able to get up close to him. Oh, my he has nice firm biceps, I almost melted when I rubbed up against him! If that nosey ex-cop Brian hadn't been there. Who knows what could have happened. I could have had my way with him I'm sure of it. I will come up with a better thought-out plan to make that happen and then he will be mine. No man can resist me.

Fergus thumbed forward until he came upon the night, she lied to get him into her apartment. *Intruder my ass! I should have known better when it came to her. She caught me when I was tired, and I fell for her bullshit.* He continued to read on.

My plan worked! My detective came to my rescue, I knew he would. I had dreamt about this moment, and it worked! It worked! I called him and pretended there was an intruder. I know he cares about me the way he rushed in to save me. Fergus realized what was going on and kissed me tenderly anyway it was so passionate. He didn't care that I tricked him. He wanted me as much as I wanted him. Especially When I pressed myself up against him, I could feel his excitement. He carried me to the bed; we removed our clothing, and he gently but firmly entered me. It was so exhilarating! I climaxed twice!

Fergus laid the diary face down on the counter. He didn't know if he should stop reading or go on. He got himself a glass of water and picked up the diary, he thumbed toward the day Lily arrived.

I went to meet up with my detective and noticed he was with another woman!

How could he just ignore me after the passionate night we had together?

Fergus, did you just use me for your own sexual gratification? Who is this woman you

brought here? She looks like a cheap tramp! She is probably a gold digger. Fergus,

What are you thinking? I slipped a note under her door. Maybe she will get the

hint and go away seeing this older man isn't worth the trouble.

Fergus stopped reading at that moment, "Lil, you were right! It was Beverly who left you that note. I'm also sure she trashed your room as well."

Fergus skimmed through a few more pages and found the part when Lily came back a second time.

Mary from housekeeping opened the room that tramp of Fergus' is staying in. I told her she was my daughter and I left something in there. Mary is new and quite naïve. I couldn't find anything out about his tart. I went through everything except the safe, it was locked. I knew Mary wouldn't open it for me no matter what I told her. I was lucky she opened the room. I played on her sympathy; she didn't want to open it up at first. I asked her 'what if it was your mother? Wouldn't you want someone to let her in?' I promised her I wouldn't be long and would lock up.

Fergus had read enough. He knew he should go back and check the time Blanche was killed to see if Beverly knew anything about that. He looked up at the clock and closed the diary. It was time to meet up with Cookie.

As he walked toward the Bistro he couldn't help thinking, *I believe Beverly could only be honest with her diary knowing she was the only one who was ever going to see it.* He shook his head in disgust. Cookie, seated at a high-top table, saw Fergus walking toward her, she smiled and waved at him.

"What's wrong?"

Fergus sat down, "Nothing why?"

"Don't you give me that mister! I know you better than you think I do. And I know that look."

"I was just thinking about my conversations with Lizabeth and Doug. That's all nothing really important." He didn't want to tell Cookie about the diary not knowing what or how she might take it.

"Aw so you found both of them. Did they have anything interesting to say?"

"No, not really. Lizabeth hated Beverly and wished her dead on several occasions. Doug heard Beverly hollering out by the pool and closed his door to shut out her drunken rant. I don't believe either of them had anything to do with her death. I am going to take the pen Lucy found to the Medical Examiner's Office and see if he can send it into the lab. Hopefully and I know it's a shot in the dark, maybe there is something, DNA, a partial print anything."

"Oh, that is such a good idea, you are so smart!"

Fergus had to laugh at Cookie's remark, "They didn't make me a detective because of my looks."

The two continued to visit over lunch. Fergus walked Cookie back to her apartment, "I'll check in with you later."

Cookie gave his arm a squeeze, "Later."

Fergus was ready to dive back into the diary. He found the part he was looking for.

I am surprised Blanche joined the windchime club. I noticed she hung chimes out on her patio during my evening walk. I've racked my brain trying to figure out who runs that darn thing. I have a couple of ideas however I will keep that to myself for now. Later that evening after the sun had already set, I noticed a tall what looked like a man, dressed in dark clothing, walking toward her apartment. I couldn't quite tell who it was. I did see that he had on white shoes, possibly loafers or tennis shoes I couldn't tell because it was dark. The following day is when Blanche was found by the housekeeping staff. I didn't mention anything to Sam about it. I'm not sure if that man even went into her apartment. When I heard she died of natural causes I let it go.

Fergus thumbed through the diary to find several entries about Sondra, Lacey and Roxie.

I don't know who Sondra thinks she is challenging me the way she does. She should know by now she will be on the losing end of things. I've had it with her! She needs to be taught a lesson or two and I'm just the one to do it!

Fergus flipped through a few more pages skimming by rants until he came upon the entry in the restaurant.

I had to give Sondra a little baptism in the restaurant this evening. I had told her to back off. That one never listens. My god! I was hoping she would melt after I threw my water on her. Ha! No such luck! I'm not finished with that one yet. She has pushed my buttons for the last time. I'm coming for you BITCH!!

Fergus shook his head, "I really dodged a bullet! Beverly you are even worse than I ever suspected."

He continues to read on.

Oh, boo hoo Sondra is dead. Hold on, let me wipe my eyes dry. Bitch you got everything you had coming. I hope the flames of hell lick your heels before you get to the gate. Here's the funny part: I do believe you will be the richest bitch in the graveyard. Ha, ha, ha! Bye, bye Bitch!!

Fergus closed the diary. There wasn't anything more about Sondra's murder after that entry. *I truly believe this woman was mentally ill. All she did was tear others down for her own entertainment. I'm surprised Sam wanted anything to do with her. Maybe he never saw her for who she actually was.*

Fergus put the diary's back. He would pass them on to Lily when he saw her. He walked over to the fridge and took out a beer, "I believe it's beer thirty. I need this after reading all of that!" He walked out toward his patio.

Chapter 29:
Birds of a Feather

It's no secret that Eugene watches his surroundings. Everyone has commented on it one time or another. The same goes for Hazel and Edna, they are aware of what goes on around them. The interesting thing about those three is they watch each other as well. The question is do they know they are watching each other? Of course, they do. Hazel and Edna noticed that long ago. Eugene has always kept a sharp eye on things around him ever since the home invasion before he moved with his wife Joan to Summers Bay. He wanted a safe place for them to live out their retirement years. Edna and Hazel liked the idea of resort style retirement.

"Hazel, I'm not going to stand here all day waiting for you. Hurry up."

"Hold your horses. Are we on a time limit or something?"

"I just want to get down to the pool, so we have a nice shady spot before they are all taken up."

"All right all ready, hold on to your britches."

"You are the slowest at times."

The sisters arrived at the pool before noon. They noticed Eugene sitting at a table with an umbrella not far from them. They acknowledged each other with a nod. Eugene with his usual book in hand would occasionally peer over the top to see who was coming into the pool area.

Roxanne was already seated on a lounge chair wearing a large sunhat. She was slathering on sunscreen when Lacey walked through the gate. Lacey lowered her sunglasses and rolled her eyes at Roxanne.

Roxanne scoffed, “They will let anyone in here, won’t they?”

Lacey put her sunglasses back in place, “I guess they will, they let you in, didn’t they?” Lacey placed her pool bag on the lounge chair next to Roxanne. She laid her towel out and sat down. Roxanne tried to ignore her. Lacey started to lather sunscreen on her legs.

Hazel and Edna looked in Eugene’s direction at the same time he looked at them. All three looked toward Roxie and Lacey.

Roxie looked at Lacey, “Are you seriously going to sit there?”

“Yes, why not? It’s open seating. Besides, you know this is the best side for sunbathing.”

Roxie got up and turned her chair at an angle so she wouldn’t have to look at Lacey.

Edna leaned toward Hazel, “I hope those two can control themselves. I came out here for relaxation, not World War three.”

Hazel nudged her sister, “Let’s have a chat with Eugene. Come on.” The two walked over to his table.

Eugene set his book down, “Yes, it’s about time we chat don’t you think?”

Edna smiled, “That is exactly what I have been thinking.”

Eugene extended his arm, “Please sit.”

Edna and Hazel looked over at Roxie and Lacey, “We know you watched the cat fight yesterday between those two.”

"I did, and I also noticed you watched as well from your apartment."

"Like you, we don't miss much." The sisters smiled at Eugene.

"I thought things might have settled down with Beverly, and Sondra gone. I guess I was wrong."

"You left out Blanche." They could hear the arguing as it was getting louder. The three of them looked in the direction toward Roxie and Lacey.

"Blanche was never a problem; she died a natural death."

Both sisters looked at each other and smiled, "If you say so."

"The medical examiner said so."

Hazel looked directly into Eugene's eyes, "You know we're not stupid."

"I don't know what you're talking about."

"Sure, you do."

"We were born, but not yesterday. We have watched you and know things that you do."

"Well, that makes us even, I've watched you two as well. I'm aware of a few things that the two of you do."

Hazel looked over at the ladies who seemed to be at each other again.

Roxanne turned to look at Lacey, "For crying out loud Lacey just move your chair away from me. I can't stand the sight of you and your fat saggy thighs."

Lacey's jaw dropped. Roxanne smiled at her own remark knowing that would get to her.

"I would rather have saggy thighs than a saggy neck! You look like a thanksgiving turkey. Gobble, gobble bitch." Lacey knew Roxanne was sensitive about her neck starting to sag with age.

Roxanne sat up and turned toward Lacey, "Why I never!"

Lacey laughed loud enough for everyone at the pool to hear, "I want those shoes back that you borrowed. They belong to me now." She said through gritted teeth.

"Over my dead body!" Roxanne laid back down on her lounge chair.

Lacey leaned forward, "I WILL get them back."

"Like I said over my dead body."

"I think that might be arranged."

Hazel whispered to Edna, "I had hoped we were finished with house cleaning."

Eugene smiled at them, "I agree with you ladies." There seemed to be a mutual understanding between the three of them.

Hazel stood, "It was nice chatting with you, let's do it again sometime."

Eugene nodded at them as they returned to their shaded area.

Roxanne had tried her best to ignore Lacey. It wasn't working. The two kept digging at each other.

Roxanne looked at Lacey, "I've been meaning to tell you, you look like a beached whale in that swimsuit. You know, too many desserts will do that, you know."

Lacey shot back, "Listen up penis breath, you're no prize either."

Edna whispered to her sister, "Which one do you think needs help with our house cleaning?'

Hazel smiled, "Maybe they both do."

Eugene looked over the top of his book, "I heard that ladies. I have a mop you can borrow." All three of them laughed.

Roxanne shot a glare at them, "WHAT'S SO FUNNY? WHY DON'T YOU MIND YOUR OWN BUSINESS?"

Hazel waved at Roxanne, "Let's offer her our services first."

Roxanne held up her middle finger at them.

Edna sent it right back. Hazel nudged her sister, "Control yourself."

Edna smiled, "Sorry sister but that felt good."

Lacey finally gave up; she picked up her things and left. Roxanne called out to her by the gate, "HEY LACEY YOU FORGET THIS." Then she held up her middle finger to her. Lacey hollered back, "SORRY YOU'RE NOT MY TYPE. OH WAIT, THAT HAS TO BE YOUR IQ." She turned and walked toward the building.

Eugene picked up his things as he walked by the sisters he smiled, "House cleaning, I like that."

They waved at him, "Hazel, let's keep an eye on that one." She nodded toward Roxanne.

"My thoughts exactly."

Chapter 30:
Cleanliness Is Next To Godliness, Is It Really?

The sisters were getting ready to go down to the restaurant for dinner. Hazel walked into the kitchen for a bottle of water, "Sister, remember our teachings from church when mom and dad made us go?"

Edna frowned, "I've tried to forget. Why bring that up?"

"Remember Matthew 23:25-28? It talks about being clean on the outside but unclean on the inside?"

"Yes, I remember that, I think. I believe it also said you must be clean from the inside out."

"You're right sister. Now think of our housecleaning. Think of us helping clean things up that look clean on the outside but are surely unclean on the inside."

Edna looked at her sister, "Are you seriously trying to make an excuse for our house cleaning? What we are cleaning up is rotten to the core! There is no other word or words to explain. It's like that old saying we have heard many times; beauty is only skin deep. That is not true, beauty comes from within."

"You left out the ending. Ugly goes all the way to the bone. Not only are those two ladies rotten to the core, they are ugly with each other which makes them ugly to the bone."

"I get what you're saying. Are you feeling guilty? That is the message you're sending me."

Hazel looked at her sister, "No, I'm not feeling guilty. I was just expressing my thoughts."

"Well, you've expressed them. Let's go eat."

As they entered the restaurant, they saw Eugene in the back at his usual table. They acknowledged each other with a nod. Roxanne was sitting over by the wall with that new man that recently moved in. Lacey walked in behind the sisters when Doug motioned for her to come to their table. Roxanne shook her head no at Lacey. Lacey walked over anyway and sat down. Roxie looked uncomfortable.

Edna nodded her head toward the three of them. Hazel looked over, "Oh please no drama. I've had enough for the day."

Roxanne's expression changed as she got up and left. Lacey smiled as she walked toward the door. Hazel looked relieved. Doug looked a bit confused as to what was going on between them.

Fergus was seated with Brian as they were just finishing up their meal. Fergus made it a point to look around the room checking out men's footwear. He noticed several men were wearing white sport or tennis shoes including Eugene. No white loafers. He was trying to watch as they came in and left checking out their height. He thought to himself, *what might be tall to Beverly might not be tall to someone else.*

Eugene wiped his mouth with his napkin then laid it on his plate. He walked by Fergus and Brian giving them a nod. Eugene was tall and fit the description Beverly wrote about in her diary. Doug also fits that description. In fact, there were several others.

Fergus thought to himself, *I wonder if Doug had bought his apartment before Blanche passed away. Could he have been there that night? That is something I will be checking out.*

Fergus' phone rang, "excuse me Brian I have to take this."

"Fergie, I have some interesting news to share with you. Can you talk?"

"Not at the moment."

"I just wanted to fill you in on the background checks."

"I'll call you back when I get home." He closed his flip phone and put it in his pocket.

"Hey Brian, I've got to return Lily's phone call. I'll catch up with you later. Thanks for meeting me for dinner."

"No problem, I'll see you later."

Fergus called Lily when he arrived back at his apartment, "Lil, what did you find out? Anything good?"

"Are you sitting down?"

"No, do I need to?"

"I have a bit of surprising news to share. Let me start with Eugene Watson."

Fergus was surprised to hear that Eugene had a last name that started with a 'W', "What did you find out?"

"A few years back before he and his wife Joan moved to Summer's Bay there was a break in at their home. It was shortly after the break in that he and his wife sold and moved into Sunset Village."

"You have my attention, I'm all ears."

"Apparently Eugene was sleeping when the break in occurred. Joan had gotten up to get a drink of water when she heard glass break.

She woke her husband in a panic. Eugene had a baseball bat he kept behind the bedroom door that he used on the intruder, he didn't survive. Eugene beat him to death."

"Wow!"

"Of course, he wasn't charged with the murder because of the castle doctrine."

"Interesting to know."

"The grandmotherly ladies have a spotless record. Edna was engaged at one time and her fiancé fell down a flight of stairs at a party, breaking his neck. Edna inherited his interest in his law firm, his home, everything he had. She and Hazel never married."

"Did you find anything on Lacey or Roxanne?"

"Oh yes. Roxanne James worked for a trucking company. Her job was to route trucks to different destinations to pick up and deliver loads. She was very good at her job, so good that when the owner's nephew who inherited the company insisted, she stay on. It was later found out she had embezzled thousands and thousands of dollars from the nephew. She was never charged. Who knows how much she embezzled and got away with. The nephew lost the business and later committed suicide."

"Good grief! How did you get that information if she wasn't charged?"

"Oh, come on Fergie! You know I have my ways. I made a call to the Burns Brothers Crematorium, they informed me." She said with a smile.

"Smart lady you are."

"Thanks, now let me tell you about Lacey Martin. This is an interesting one. She had been involved with several men. She always seemed to pick bad boys. They took advantage of her. She has been a victim of abuse ever since she was a child. She spent time in jail a few years back for poisoning one of her boyfriends. She claimed it was self-defense. There was a trial and long story short she got off on time served."

Fergus rubbed his chin, "Those are just the ones you checked out? Makes me wonder who else is living or hiding out here."

Lily laughed, "I will not run a check on everyone who lives there Fergie. While I was there visiting, I looked around at the residents, out at the pool, in the restaurant and at the party. My thought was everyone has a story and I just found out how true that is."

"I have a bit of news for you."

"Yeah, hit me."

"Cookie dropped in for coffee and Lucy was running around like she usually does when she first gets here. She was in my bedroom closet digging at something she found back in the corner."

"What did she find?"

"Interesting enough a black pen with the initials E. W. printed in white. Now who does that sound like?"

"Eugene? I just told you his last name is Watson! Oh my! Fergie! Madame Yvette was right!"

"I'm taking it over to the M.E.'s office to see if they can find anything on it."

"I also read Beverly's diaries." There was a long pause.

"And? Don't tell me she confessed everything to her diary?"

"You could say that."

"Fergie! That is wonderful!"

"Hold on, there isn't anything about the windchime club. She didn't run it. In fact, she didn't like it. She did mention she had a couple of ideas about who was in charge of it but never put it in the diary. She did witness someone walking in the direction of Blanche's apartment the night before they found her. That person wore dark clothing with white loafers or tennis shoes and seemed tall to her."

"Eugene!"

"Maybe, I'm not sure. It's all circumstantial. I was watching men come in and out of the restaurant and we have a complex filled with male suspects."

"Fergie, what about the pen?"

"Maybe Blanche borrowed it, she was friendly with him. She knew and liked his wife."

"Beverly cheered Sondra's death in her diary. I'll pass them to you when you head back this way."

"That will be sooner than you might expect. I'll keep you posted."

"I think we are getting close to finding out some truths."

Chapter 31:
Pies and Lies

Fergus invited Cookie to take a drive to Ocean City for the afternoon. Cookie was excited she had been wanting to check out a new clothing store that had recently opened.

Fergus looked over at Cookie in the passenger's seat, "I'm going to make a stop and drop off the pen that Lucy found."

"That's fine, I'm curious to hear what if anything is found on it."

"That makes two of us."

Fergus parked, "I'll be right out, this will just take a minute."

"No worries, I'll be waiting." She said with a smile. Cookie reached into her purse for her lipstick. She pulled the visor down to look in the mirror as she touched up her lips. No sooner had she finished, when Fergus opened the car door. "That was quick."

"Yep."

"Doc will let me know as soon as the results come in."

The drive to Ocean City was scenic, it took about twenty-five minutes. The road was a little windy. Their conversation was light and pleasant. They truly enjoyed being around each other.

Fergus parked in front of Candy's Sweet Shop. The storefront was painted pink with purple trim around the large windows on each side of the double doors. The windows were trimmed with white lights on the inside. The front doors were old-fashioned dark wood with glass panes. A metal sign hung on the side of one of the big windows with a picture of a wrapped candy on the top of the sign, underneath it read, "Candy's Sweet Shop."

Cookie looked at Fergus, "Are we going in?"

"Yes, we are. I've heard about this place and have been wanting to check it out."

Fergus opened and held the door for Cookie. The smell of freshly baked goods was heavenly. Cookie walked up to the counter checking out the array of cookies, donuts, pies, and breads on one side of the counter. On the other side was fudge, toffees, brittles, caramel and candied apples. There was a refrigerator section with cakes. "OOOH Fergie look at this carrot cake! I love carrot cake."

Fergus walked over to peek, "I believe I've tasted that before. It was delicious."

"Really when was that?"

Just then a cheerful lady wearing a pink apron came out of the kitchen behind the counter and she looked in their direction, "Good afternoon I'm Candy may I help you?"

Fergus walked up to the counter, "I'm curious do you sell many pies and cakes? They look delicious. "I'm sure I have tasted your carrot cake before."

"You might have. Where are you from?"

"Summers Bay."

Candy smiled at Fergus, "There seems to be run-on cookies, cakes, and pies every so often. Several ladies from Summers Bay come in and clean me out." She said with a laugh that was infectious.

Fergus rubbed his chin, "Interesting."

"I don't ask questions; I am happy to make the sales. Would you like a sample of peanut butter fudge?"

Cookie walked over to the counter, "I would please."

Candy opened the front case; she cut two pieces of fudge and placed them on a small square of paper.

Cookie was in fudge heaven, "Oh my! This is heavenly! I would like a half pound of that."

Fergus agreed, "This is delicious. You make all this by yourself?"

Candy laughed out loud, "Heavens no! I have plenty of help. The recipes come from my family. I helped in the kitchen as a child. My favorite things to make were always sweets."

Candy handed Cookie her fudge, "Enjoy."

"Oh, we will."

Cookie thanked Candy as Fergus held the door for her. Candy waved from behind the counter with her big smile, "I'll see you next time."

The two of them walked down the sidewalk checking out the store fronts. Cookie went into a women's clothing store, while Fergus sat on a bench outside holding the bag of fudge. He reached inside for another piece. After about fifteen minutes Cookie walked out carrying a bag. Fergus stood, "looks like you found something."

Cookie smiled, "I did. I have had my eye on a couple of items that had been advertised."

The two spent the afternoon in Ocean City checking out the small stores, "Fergie, I want to tell you I've had a wonderful day."

"Well good, that was the idea. Let's get a bite to eat before heading back."

Fergus had noticed Don's café on their way into town, "Let's stop at that café on our way back we saw earlier."

Cookie saw the neon sign as they got closer, "Don's? It looks quaint. Shopping has given me an appetite."

They were seated in a window booth. Cookie couldn't hold back, "When did you taste Candy's carrot cake?"

Fergus touched Cookie's hand from across the table, "Remember when I first moved in?"

Cookie said with a laugh, "How could I not!"

"All those ladies, well let's say most of them brought me housewarming gifts of food they said they made from scratch. I now know it all came from Candy's Sweet Shop."

Cookie nearly choked on her iced tea, "They told you they made them from scratch?"

Fergus nodded, "Yes, they did."

"Why those conniving liars! That is just too funny!"

"Candy told me every so often she gets a run on her baked goods from ladies that come in from Summer's Bay."

Cookie shook her head, "Beverly must have orchestrated that, I'm sure."

Fergus set his menu down, "You're probably right."

Fergus and Cookie laughed and enjoyed their meal. The drive back was beautiful, the sun was setting and the colors in the sky were pink and purple just like Candy's Sweet Shop.

Fergus walked Cookie to her door. He kissed her on her cheek, "I'll see you tomorrow for coffee?"

"You will."

Fergus could hear Lucy inside happily greeting Cookie.

Chapter 32:
No Sales, No Commission

Sunset Village had been close to capacity however things have changed since the three deaths. Residents were worried that a serial killer might live among them. Residents were moving out and putting their condo's up for sale. Moving trucks were a usual sight by the side of the building. Renters were giving their notice.

Malissa, the in-house realtor, was busy listing condos for sale. Prices had fallen, however that wasn't a problem for her. She worked on commission. Tragedy has a way of driving prices down. No sales, no commission. The local news cast spooked more residents. A day didn't go by without someone asking, "Are we safe here? What security measures were being taken." Malissa always tried to assure residents that safety was a priority. She also reminded them to lock their doors, "Until someone is arrested, we need to watch out for one another." She then would smile which made some think she was enjoying the chaos. Roxie was furious with Malissa for selling Sondra's condo to Lacey without consulting her. Roxie saw her at the front desk and decided to confront her about it. Malissa saw her walking toward her out of the corner of her eye. *Oh, brother, I knew this was going to happen sooner or later.* She braced herself for hurricane Roxie.

"Malissa, I have a bone to pick with you!" she sternly said.

"Really? Let me guess what it's about…Humm…could this be about you losing out on Sondra's condo?"

"You knew I wanted to purchase that unit! Why would you not contact me and let me know what was going on?"

"Because dear like I said before money talks."

"I could have counter offered; you didn't give me a chance."

"Listen Roxie, it's just business, nothing personal. Lacey offered me more for that unit than it was worth. I wasn't going to pass that up. Besides, I don't think you could have matched what she paid for it."

Roxie was seething, "You have no idea how much money I have, or what I could have paid. Thanks for nothing!" She turned and walked away.

Malissa was relieved she left. She knew that one could be aggressive and loud. She kept busy the rest of the day with appointments writing up sales contracts. She decided to advertise in newspapers away from Summers Bay. The deaths had only been on local news. Knowing she needed to entice retirees to move she offered a move in special, free covered parking space for the first six months.

The following week

Cookie came back from the grocery store, she needed food and treats for Lucy and a half gallon of her favorite ice cream, mint chip. As she was getting out of her car, she noticed Malissa getting into a red Tesla. *Wow! Looks like Malissa is riding in style.* She couldn't hear the car start up. *Oh, it's one of those expensive electric cars. Malissa must have a sugar daddy or business has been good to her. Very interesting.*

Lucy was excited to get one of her favorite treats from her mama, "You be a good girl. I'll be right back."

She knocked on Fergus' door and he opened it with a smile, "Hey, come in."

"Fergie, you are never going to believe what I just saw in the parking lot!"

Fergus was intrigued, "Tell me! This must be good."

"Oh, it's good alright, Malissa is driving a new red Tesla!"

"Really? She must have come into some money."

"I'll say! If you ask me, she is double dipping on condo sales. People buy in, then they get spooked and sell them. She is making commission hand over fist!"

"It almost sounds illegal."

"I know right! I think she is sly like a fox! I almost think she made this happen."

"How so?" Fergus poured them both a glass of wine.

"Think about it. Blanche passes away. Natural they say. Some think otherwise. Then Sondra is murdered. Beverly is floating in our pool outside for everyone to see. People panic, move out, sell their apartments and Malissa profits."

"I'd hate to think that however, it's an interesting thought. You might be onto something." Fergus rubbed his chin, he's always done that when he is thinking.

"Movement around this place has been crazy. I've noticed some new faces checking this place out. It's mostly married couples moving out. Only a few singles and those are women."

"I can understand single women feeling unsafe. How are you feeling about all of this."

"Oh, I'm not worried. Lucy is a good watch dog. Besides, I've got you close by and that makes me feel safe."

"I really don't think you have anything to worry about. It seems that targets have been on loud aggressive women with Blanche excluded. I thought Beverly might have killed Sondra there for a while. I don't believe that to be so anymore."

"What made you change your mind?"

"The more I've learned about both women, they actually enjoyed sparring with each other. Beverly would rather humiliate you in front of a crowd. Her tongue was her weapon, and she knew how to use that."

"It's such a beautiful day, let's go out to the patio. We can people watch while we sip our wine."

"Sounds like a plan. With all the happenings around here, we need to recharge."

They carried their wine glasses outside and sat until the sun started to set. Conversation was never dull between the two of them.

Medical Examiner calls

Fergus answered his phone, "Fergus here."

"Good afternoon, Fergus, I have results for you from the ink pen."

"Hey doc, anything good I hope?"

"Unfortunately, no it was smudged so there were no prints. There was male DNA but not enough to come up with anything concrete. I'm sorry I don't have better news for you."

"I wasn't expecting much, I knew it would be a longshot."

"Good idea to run it through the lab, you never know."

"Thanks Doc." He closed his flip phone and laid it on the counter.

He knew there was nothing more than circumstantial evidence with Blanche's death. Nothing to point at anyone specific. The pen was hopeful especially with the initials the same as Eugene Watson. There is no proof he was there and dropped it. What Beverly wrote in her diary matched just about every man in the village. Blanche's death would stay natural causes, due to a heart attack. The detective in Fergus told him Eugene was the cause of her death.

Fergus decided it was time to call Lily and fill her in on everything he had found out.

Lily was still at her desk in Springfield when her phone rang, "Go for Lily."

"Hey Lil, I hope I didn't catch you at a bad time."

"Actually, I'm just finishing up. I was getting ready to head home. Have you found anything else out over there?"

"I have some ideas. The lab just found male DNA on the pen, no prints. Cookie thinks Malissa is cashing in on the deaths. I'm inclined to agree with her."

"Interesting, so that pen belonged to Eugene at one time."

"I think he contributed to Blanche's death. Remember Doc said she was scared to death. I think he scared her, and the dildo was an afterthought."

"What about Beverly? We know she was poisoned. I think our sweet little ladies might know more about that."

"They made Oliver dinner, possibly to see if he knew anything while they visited and pretended to be her best friends."

"Nothing points to them other than opportunity."

"Then we have Sondra. You noticed the button missing on one of the little ladies' blouses. There was white hair that was found which had to be transferred; there were no roots attached. It could have come from anyone around here."

"Fergie, do you think those little ladies could have killed Sondra?"

"I think it's possible, especially with her sitting on the bed putting on her shoes. One shoe is on, she is holding the other shoe. Let's say one of the ladies grabs the trophy, hits her from behind and the other picks up the shoe and 'BAM'!"

"Sounds like that could have happened that way. However, we have no evidence to pin it on them."

"Lil, I think this is one of those cases that is going to go unsolved. We may think we know what has gone on here. I guess we will have to wait and see if someone, sometime slips up."

"I hope whoever is responsible stops while they are ahead."

"Since I moved here, I have continued to work. I've really enjoyed it. I've worked on my time. With that said, I've decided to take the state's private investigators exam."

"Oh Fergie, really?" Lily says with excitement.

"Yes, I already have my carry permit. I will work on cases that I want on my time."

"That's wonderful! What cases are you thinking you will be taking on?"

"I'm thinking along the lines of missing persons, theft, insurance fraud, cheating spouses, lost dogs, that kind of stuff. I might even deliver papers for the courts."

"Keep me posted when you pass your exam. I've been working on a few missing persons cases here. I could really use some help if you're interested."

"Let me pass the exam first and we will talk about it."

"I'm excited for you. I'll check in with you later."

Fergus closed his flip phone and laid it on the counter.

Cookie looked surprised at what Fergus had to say, "Where do I fit in?"

"You are going to be my assistant and help me with my record keeping if you're interested."

"When you say assistant, do you mean we will go on stake outs together?"

"That is exactly what I mean, what do you think?"

"I'm very interested, do I get a code name?"

A smile escaped the corners of his mouth, "Of course you get a code name, I wouldn't have it any other way."

Epilogue

Fergus passed his exam and became a licensed private detective. He took on a few small cases. One actually was a lost dog. He made a trip to Springfield with Cookie to check out the missing persons cases Lily had been working on. He decided to work with Lily on a few of them.

Cookie and Fergus continued to see each other exclusively. They each kept their own condos. Cookie was a great assistant to Fergus; they worked well together.

Brian had his barber girlfriend move in with him. There was talk of marriage.

Malissa was the one who sent the letter to Andrea Day. Her advertising worked; she was selling condos left and right. New residents were moving in. Sunshine Village was filling up once again.

Edna and Hazel continued to keep an eye on things including Eugene. They noticed a new couple that had moved in. The woman stood out because she wore blonde wigs all the time, she dressed like she was a teenager and flirted with men when her husband wasn't around. Her husband got the job of driving the Village bus taking residents to doctors appointments and to local stores. The woman had a fake smile like Beverly. The sisters decided she was someone worth keeping an eye on for now anyway.

Lacey moved into Sondra's apartment. She was in heaven, Sondra's shoes fit her, and her clothes were the right size too. Roxie still hadn't returned the shoes. Lacey wasn't going to let that go.

Roxie made friends with that blonde woman with the fake smile. They joined the karaoke club together. She wore the shoes she borrowed from Sondra every chance she got. She and Lacey never reconciled.

Eugene was the one who made the phone calls, he was sending out a warning. He continued to do what he had always done, watch. He read his books out by the pool. He was happy as long as there was no drama.

Sheriff Sam never tried to investigate the deaths. They remain unsolved to this day. He retired and moved to Sunshine Village. He became popular with the single ladies.

The windchime club was disbanded. It was never discovered who started that up.

With there being more single women than men. There will always be jealousy among some of the women. The single men seemed to enjoy the attention they were getting.

Doug Howard played the field like the rest of them. He dated Lacey a few times. He always seemed to come up with flirty lines for the women. Even Edna and Hazel enjoyed his playfulness.

Gary Hart lived a low-profile life. He dated a few of the single ladies, nothing serious.

Kelly and Doc Thompson continued to work at the Medical Examiner's Office. It seemed that they liked their work. Business, as Doc Thompson called it, was slow and they liked it that way.

Made in the USA
Las Vegas, NV
08 November 2023

80056975R00144